A Buddha *in the* Study

NITISH SINHA

INDIA · SINGAPORE · MALAYSIA

ISBN
Paperback 979-8-89446-300-1
Hardcase 979-8-89475-259-4

Disclaimer

This is a work of fiction set against a background of history. Public personages, both living and dead, may appear in the story under their given names. Scenes and dialogues involving them are invented. Any resemblance of the fictional characters to real persons, living or dead, is entirely coincidental. No claim regarding historical accuracy is either made or implied. Historical, religious, or mythological characters, events, or places are always used fictitiously.

Dedicated to the memory of

Manish Kumar,

My Cousin and My Alter Ego

Contents

1

A Buddha in the Study

I developed a fondness for Mahakashyap, the most revered monk among the followers of Gautam Buddha, but never had a desire to invite him into my study.

"Okay. Let it be. Just for the sake of discussion, now I am accepting for a while that you are the same person you are claiming to be."

"My pleasure," he smiles.

It seems Lord Buddha was smiling on his face! I smiled back.

"Now you are Mahakashyap, the chief disciple of the same Gautam Buddha who lived around 500 BC, precisely between 569 BC and 489 BC, according to the available records. The same Buddha who got married at 16, left home at the age of twenty-nine for salvation, achieved Nirvana at 35, and died at eighty after living the life of an ascetic and giving sermons all over," I said, eyeing the person sitting cross-legged in front of me, on my cot beside my reading table. The same table on which there was a statue of Buddha, not less than 12 inches in height. I had purposely placed the statue on a heavy volume of Dhammapada to give it good balance. This statue was a birthday gift from someone who knows well about my obsession with Buddha.

"I am not sure about these numbers like 569, 489, 16, 29, or 35, dear Anand Kumar. I wonder how you all are so sure about these numbers concerning a person who lived so long ago. Even I am not sure about such numbers about my lord even during that time," said the self-proclaimed Mahakashyap, who was once the chief disciple of Buddha. He was dressed in the same attire as described in Buddhist scriptures, called chiwar, a three-piece, near-to-orange coloured dress. The dress was exceptionally old but clean. Even the hairstyle had a striking similarity to the statue of his teacher sitting beside him. The only difference was the colour; the statue was black, and the person was fair.

Oh! If this person were really Mahakashyap, then this chiwar must be the original chiwar of Gautam Buddha! Isn't it written that Buddha replaced his chiwar with that of Mahakashyap?

But only if this person is the same one!

But again, the same obvious thought came into my mind: how did this Bhikkhu enter my study room? Nobody is supposed to enter here without my permission. Not even Buddha! Or maybe my mum allowed him to enter my study during my absence! Or is this a dream? And he knows my name.

I should have been surprised by his presence in my room, but now I am not. This surprises me. Everything seems normal to me. And I replied,

"I see what you mean. Even I have heard that some Chinese traditions put his life around 1000 BC. In the Kalachakra tradition, he lived around 900 BC. But 569 BC and 489 BC are widely accepted timelines."

"I wonder if this sort of timeline is important. Even the Tathagat never showed any interest in such things."

"But in today's world, it is damn important, at least for an Aadhaar card," I smile.

"And what is this?"

"A sort of proof of identity if you are Indian. But I don't think this has any importance for you. But still, numbers have importance."

"Yeah. Sometimes it has when I started counting my steps or counting my breath just for the sake of meditation. But earlier you had mentioned the word 'Kalachakra.' Kalachakra! Oh, that word really attracts me!"

"Me too! Recently I read a thriller about that. Even I read somewhere that Buddha passed that knowledge of Kalachakra to some king of Shambhala."

"Another interesting word, Shambhala! So, you really are a knowledgeable person, I suppose."

I feel elated. I just got praised by the chief disciple of Buddha. If he was.

"I am not sure about my intelligence. But Buddha always attracts me, especially his idols. His sitting postures. He always looks so handsome."

"Just like some Roman gods."

I didn't understand the comparison.

"Idol worship was not his forte. He always decried such things. I wonder how such things started. It is shameful if one person idolises another."

"It is just a way to express your love for him. But yes, I have heard or read that he was a non-believer. And he avoided questions regarding God or Souls."

He smiles fully.

"One of the nearest persons to Tathagat is sitting in front of you. And you are trying to inform me what he says or what he thinks."

"No, I just want to say what people think…"

But he was telling the truth. One of the most important disciples of Buddha is sitting in front of me, and I was just trying to show how clever I am.

But how am I believing that the original Mahakashyap is sitting here, in my study? Isn't it sheer nonsense on my part? Why am I believing in unbelievable things? A person who is supposed to be around 2500 years old. How on earth...

"Actually, Buddha is the person who attracts me as he never deviated to unnecessary things. But when I read scriptures dedicated to him, lots of doubts came into my mind. And Buddha is not here to clear them."

But for a matter of fact, Mahakashyap fascinates me most these days.

"Now you are on the correct path," he laughs. "Doubt is certain, and it is not a sin. In Buddhist thought, there is nothing like sin as is in other religions. During his lifetime, Tathagat was always there to clear our doubts. Even moments before his death, he asked several times if anybody had any doubts about his teachings. But if you are doubting something just to oppose something, then it will lead you nowhere. Therefore, always keep trying to dispel your doubts. And after his death, we have collected the Tripitaka for the same purpose. Everything is there." I could see his toothless jaws. He continues,

"Tathagat always says not to believe anything, even if it was told by him. Believe nothing, no matter where you read it or who has said it, no matter even if it had been told by Tathagat himself unless it agrees with your own reason and your common sense."

"I wonder if our prejudiced common sense is clear enough to believe something."

"So, you have to practise Vipassana for a clear mind," the self-proclaimed Mahakashyap told me.

"I am practising it, sir, for a while, observing the breath. But a question always remains: what is the proof that it was told by Tathagat himself?" Now, I am using the word 'Tathagat'.

"Because this statement is part of the Tripitaka, the original treatise of his statements. It was collected during the first council just after the Parinirvana of Tathagat. Everything was done in front of me and, of course, with the help of Anand, Upali, and other bhikkhus."

"And it all started when someone said after the death of Tathagat that now they are free to follow their own heart as now Buddha is not available to control them. So, it was decided to collect his teachings properly. There is nothing new about this story. All these stories are available everywhere. And even if it could be believed that the Tripitaka was collected just after his death, how is it possible that his Bhikkhu Anand memorised everything correctly? In the modern world, it is possible through recording machines. But in those days, there were no such facilities." I completed my statement and gave a triumphant look at him.

He closed his eyes. Maybe he was not expecting such strong resistance from me. After all, I had done my master's in philosophy. He should have known that.

There was complete silence in the room for some time. Maybe he was searching for some answers. After a while, he opened his eyes.

"If you are a seeker of truth, it doesn't matter where the truth is coming from, whether it is from the Geeta, Upanishads, Bible, or from the Tripitaka," I stared at him. He continued,

"Believe nothing. Even if it has been told by Tathagat himself. Tathagat said so. So, setting aside my identity for a while, why not start a conversation with some statement? You can choose any statement from the Tripitaka. Even if you think that it was not originally by Tathagat."

"It sounds good," I said. "I am not a master on this subject, but I have read outlines of his teachings which are known as the core of his teachings. I studied Buddhism as a subject. And it is written everywhere."

"You mean the Four Noble Truths, I suppose. The first sermon of the Tathagat. The Dhammacakkappavattana Sutta or Dharmachakraparivartana Sutra, as you may call it," he pronounced these complicated words very well.

"Yeah, the same. The truth of suffering, its cause, and so on."

"Not suffering. It is Dukkha. Both differ. Dukkha, Samudaya, Nigrodha, and Magga. The Four Noble Truths as is told."

"So, there is dukkha. No sukkha, I suppose. These are told in Pali, the old language, the language used during his time. And these words were first told to five monks who were his earlier companions. So, it happens that after attaining Nirvana he directly went searching for his earlier companions and located them at Sarnath or Isipatana as earlier known, and gave them the four magical words because no one else was interested in hearing him," I expressed my knowledge confidently.

"Who else would understand a person of the stature of Tathagat. That's why first Tathagat spent seven weeks in seclusion without talking to anybody."

"So, Devatas asked him to come out of the inner world," I smiled mockingly.

"Who else but noble souls would make such requests," he smiled without taking account of my wit. "And surely, these five were not the first to get his attention and be addressed by the Tathagat."

"Yeah, after all, Sarnath is miles away from Bodh Gaya. Lots of people would have seen his radiating presence on the way," I have fantasised about Buddha walking barefoot many times, and it always mesmerised me.

"I can't say anything about lots of people, but I am sure about the one who crossed the path of Tathagat and was not impressed with his way." Now he was serious. All the wrinkles on his face were now blooming with radiance.

"And who was that one?" I always wonder if it was easy for him to start conveying his message without oppositions. I always feel love for Buddha, and this love was strictly for the historical Buddha, if it was possible to strain out the historical one from all the stories and gossips.

"It was Anand who crossed the path of Buddha first when he came out of solitude and wasn't impressed at all."

"Anand!" I have heard that grand old Mahakashyap had lots of differences with his closest disciple Anand and scolded him on many occasions. Anand also happened to be his personal assistant until his death. "But he came to him much later," I said.

"Sir, I am not talking about Anand, Tathagat's first cousin. I am talking about Anand Kumar, now the son of Sri Khaitan Kumar. It is another matter that he was known by a different name during the period of Tathagat."

"I don't know what you are telling, sir..." I started to say but froze suddenly. He was mentioning me. And he was telling that I, Anand Kumar, was present during Buddha's time. And not only present but also met him, confronting him.

2

History vs Fiction

"Interesting read. I like it," she said, blinking her eyes.

I stared at her. Oh, she was beautiful. Deepa Kamal, my coach, my mentor, and probably my love. I was not sure about this last paraphrase. She was a bit older than me and for me, she was the last word on Buddhism. And I am doing my thesis under her. She was my guide and still always friendly to me, and I had just presented a paper with the heading, 'A Buddha in the Study' neatly written in my handwriting to her.

"So, Mr. Anand, instead of finalising your thesis, you started writing fiction. Still, a good attempt. I am impressed, especially the part where you make yourself part of history."

I know she always loves talking to me. Meanwhile, Raju brings coffee for us. He was Madam Deepa's younger brother and always enjoyed our discussions. It was a Friday evening, and we were sitting in the drawing cum study room of my guide Deepa Kamal. She happens to be a Reader in Ancient History at the University and lives in the

Government Quarters. Sometimes I use her personal library for my thesis, and she had no objections.

"Hello, Raj. Your 12th board is due next month, and you are still smiling. I really love this confidence of your generation," he smiles back.

"Fear is there, Bhaiyya. Even doing meditation as you told."

"So, it is not helping, dear?"

"It helps, Brother. When I do meditation, fear and anxiety wash away, but it is no help for my syllabus. All fear returns when I open my books."

"I promised you that meditation will help you overcome fear. And for the syllabus, nothing will help except study and study."

"This is really some news for me that my brother is doing meditation, and you are guiding him," Deepa said.

"Don't blame me for it. You know your brother has been visiting Bodh Gaya every Sunday for a long time, and so he starts loving Buddha and meditation," I replied.

"Oh, then you should have some expert opinion on Gautam Buddha by now."

"Sure, Didi. Especially about his leaving home. I am sure Buddha left his house just to escape his board exams and nothing else."

We laugh.

"I like this new angle. Even I was searching for some new angle for that."

"Then why not make it a part of your thesis, RK? A new discovery: Siddhartha Gautam left his palace not to attain Nirvana or for any political reasons, but just to avoid the pressure from his father to clear the board exams."

"Also, add that this theory is based on the latest findings by Mr Rajkamal, who is still among his boards. Then we also have to find whether a board or any such type of exam was prevailing during that period."

"If a board was not at that time, boredom must have been there. And if boredom persists anywhere, anybody could be forced to escape," Raj said.

I looked at him astonishingly. I didn't expect such intelligent statements from him.

He continued, "I am bored with study and want to escape, and Buddha may have been bored with his palace and wealth, so he escaped."

"Rajan must be bored with me, and he escapes," added my mentor.

Suddenly, the room was shrouded with grief.

"I didn't mean that, Didi," Raj said after some time.

"I know, Bhai. But I think you are correct. Buddha may have been bored with his wife," she said in a lighter way.

"But he won her after so much fanfare. So, chances are very dim for that. But really, I liked the boredom concept."

"Really, Bhai? Then my name must be added to your thesis."

I smiled.

"Siddhartha must have been bored with the monotony of life. The same type of things daily. Every type of pleasure was with him, and therefore he gets bored..."

"I'm not impressed with your statement, AK. If such things happen, all princes and kings should be in the forest searching for enlightenment. And what would you do with the story of seeing the deprived, old, and sick for the first time?"

"Yeah, there are versions of this story. But it could be said that such visuals distracted him from the world."

"Or he gets bored with the world," added Raj.

"Also, there was the political angle of escape as mentioned by a writer."

"No AK, I don't think so. After going to the jungle, he started meeting with ascetics and gurus. Therefore, there's no need to escape from the fact that he left his family and palace in search of the ultimate truth. He would have tried practices in the palace, and when he found that his daily routines and family were barriers to achieving his supreme goal, he left."

"Somewhere it is also told by him that he was a spoiled brat. I don't know if this could be correct."

"Many things have been written, AK. If you want to work on the historical Buddha, better depend on the earliest records as later biographies depend only on dramatic narratives. Some narratives depict his father as a Suryavamshi monarch from the Ikshvaku clan or another story of Asita arriving at his birth ceremony and announcing the arrival of a Chakravartin. But as a student of history, we could write anything but with the backing of scriptures or edicts. And there are lots of scriptures; we must work very carefully. A myth with the backing of historical proofs could become history, and a history based just on mythological work is merely a myth. As our ancients were not good date keepers, our work becomes tedious."

"It means, Didi, if we have no supportive documents for any event, that event is not historical!"

"That may be history, dear, but that could not be part of our history book," I said. "Just like Ashoka was a king 200 years ago but became Ashoka the Great after some discoveries. Better understand it like this: if I see you dating a girl, this may be a fact but could not be history without proof."

"And if you have a recording of my date and you show it to my Didi, then I will be history," the boy said in a naughty tone.

There was another round of laughter.

"There is mythology, there is history, and there is history with proof. Also, there is something called historical fiction, which is the most important concept nowadays. Every eight out of ten writers are trying to write their own history using our mythological books."

"But what is wrong with this," this was always a hot topic of discussion between us, "our holy books are written in such a way that there could be hundreds of interpretations..."

"And what about history, AK?" Discussing pseudo-history always made her aggressive, "How could there be a hundred interpretations for a single event? There could be discussions whether the Pandavas were more religious or the Kauravas were less so. But history is always one, and these new-age writers are always searching for new angles and making this one more myth. And as a history student, you must stick to the facts and not try to work on new angles of fiction."

"But why are you calling this a work of fiction? Is it historically incorrect? Was Mahakashyap not the chief disciple of Buddha? Or the timeline?" I asked mischievously.

"Everything is correct, AK," she preferred to address me as AK, "Even I am impressed with your knowledge about 'Upaka'. But I am not impressed with you quoting yourself as a new incarnation of Upaka."

As we were conversing, Raj picked up my handwritten pages and started reading them.

"But who was he?" I expressed my genuine ignorance.

"Oh, at least you should know. Upaka was quoted as the first person who came across Gautam Buddha after attaining Nirvana and who hadn't shown any interest in Buddha's middle path."

"Nice. So, Hesse's Siddhartha was not the only such person..."

"Again, don't mix fiction with history. We may not be sure about Upaka's historicity, but Hesse's Siddhartha is surely a fictional character."

"Still, this fictional work attracts many Westerners towards the original works of Buddha. And there is a reason why I wrote these about Mahakashyap and made you read it."

"And what is the reason?"

"Because every bit of words written by me is real and it is not a work of fiction. It happens and it is happening."

Raj had just finished reading the paper and joined his sister who was staring at me. I knew that it was almost impossible to make her believe what I had written. Still, I was interested in completing this impossible task. To my amazement, she said,

"OK, tell me about how it happens and how it all starts."

I was not expecting this from her. I expected that she would make fun of me or scold me for writing such things. But instead, she was ready to hear my story. However, I wanted to make her read instead of just listening to me. I forwarded her another bunch of papers that I brought with me.

3

How It All Begins

This was a Wednesday evening. You may call it a Budhavar in Hindi, but for me, it becomes Buddhavar. If I am not wrong, Buddhavar is the day devoted to the Mercury God, Budha, the son of the Moon God, Chandra. Lots of stories are there in our mythology regarding the birth of Budha, which could interest a few new-age writers. Here, I want to constrain myself to Gautam the Buddha, on whom I am doing my PhD. My thesis is not on his life, but it relates, as my topic is 'Political Impact of Buddha's Teaching on Mahajanapadas During the Fifth Century BC' So, it relates. For starters, for those who are not students of history, Gautam Buddha was a prince during the sixth century BC who left his palace after his marriage and became the father of a son, became an adept, and then attained Nirvana, the supreme truth, after many austerities. Even after more than 2500 years since his passing, he is one of the most sought-after personalities, and his middle-way path attracts generations. And for the word Nirvana, you may put this word as a synonym for Moksha, another Bharatiya word for supreme truth. You will find this word in Hindu scriptures as well as in Jainism and Buddhism. Gautam Buddha may have used the word 'Nibbana', which is the Pali equivalent. For the English equivalent, you may use Enlightenment, or better, even Nirvana, as I think Oxford has already accepted this word! Literally, it means 'be extinguished' or 'blown away'. If you ask Buddha (or consult his scriptures, which are available in abundance), he may say it is 'a state without suffering'.

Why am I talking so much about this word? Since the dawn of the early twentieth century, this word has attracted so many people to India compared to any other word. Yes, this is the sheer truth that a word can attract people and drive them crazy! Now add yoga, meditation, and guru to the list. But if you ask me, Gautam Buddha was the real driving force for all seekers.

Again, why am I talking so much about Nirvana? Whenever I think of Buddha, the second word that joins my mind is the concept of Nirvana. Even today, every guru who has a large following has proclaimed that he has already attained Moksha or Nirvana!

Forgive me for being so talkative. So much reading on the topic these days makes me so. Meet anyone who is doing a thesis, and he will bring up his subject whether you discuss any alien subject. But let me return to Wednesday evening.

I had just returned from another of my daily library tours as the clock struck six. This was just like any other day, but the evening was surely not.

I entered my flat, no. 105. The door was open as usual, and my mom was busy with a new novel, as usual. Yes, she was a reading enthusiast, unlike any other lady of her age. We smiled at each other as usual.

"You are late, AK. I have been waiting for evening tea."

Three things I want to clear up: Mom started calling me AK when she heard my guide calling me by the same title. The second thing, the evening tea was my duty for years, and I always loved taking my self-made evening tea with my mom. And third, I was not late, but it was usual for her to call me late.

After tea and some silly discussions, I proceeded to my study room. [Any time she never forgets to ask about Deepa, and this was not out of her love. She was sceptical about my over-aged and divorced guide and my relationship with her. I always struggled to affirm that there was nothing like that. And these lines were not from the usual draft I forwarded to my guide to read.]

Although this room serves the purpose of a reading-cum-bedroom-cum-eating room, I affectionately called it a study room or simply study. There was a large reading table with some disarranged books, a hardbound heavy volume of Dhammapada, and a cross-legged statue of Buddha sitting on it. Beside the table, there was an extra single cot which served the purpose of seating when my friends joined me in the study.

I proceeded to the double bed, which I still used as a single. It was usual for me to take a nap in the evening for an hour or two after my day's schedule. Soon, I was enjoying my dreams.

I was not sure how I came out of my slumber. Someone was either calling my name, or I felt the presence of another. Yes, there was a monk sitting on the cot in front of my bed. Was it a dream? The room was locked from the inside. Had it been locked by me?

I raised my head to the wall clock. It was 20 minutes past 7. So, I had slept for more than 40 minutes, and this was not a dream! Oh, it was not a dream!

I jumped out of bed and charged towards the stranger with an open-mouthed voice, "Who... Who are you? What are you doing in my room?"

"Please don't shout, Anand. I am no stranger. You know me well," he told me in a calm voice.

Suddenly, I calmed down. Could he be an invited guest of my mother? A person from the Ramakrishna Mission, I suppose. My mother was a frequent visitor there. And he knew my name.

"Take your seat, Anand Kumar. You will like talking to me."

"Are you from the mission, sir?"

"No, I am not from a mission or missionary. But certainly, on a mission," he told me with his usual calmness.

Maybe he came here for some donations, and my mother sent him to me?

"But you should enter any room after knocking and taking permission or somebody from my house permits you here?"

"It always happens that we start guessing even when the answer is always in front of us. Don't need so much guesswork when I am here to answer. I am a monk and a follower of Tathagat. I came here to meet you."

"Oh, so you are a Buddhist. Then you surely were sent by my guide. I told her many times that I wanted to meet some serious followers of Buddhism. Or were you sent by Sheetal?" I was discussing her today in the library, and she told me that she had met a group of Buddhist monks days ago. I hope she contacted them and informed them about my interest.

"But why does it require a mediator to meet a Buddhist? Visit Bodh Gaya, Dharamshala, Jiranga, or any such places, and you will find them."

"Yeah, I visited Dharamshala last year, but I am more interested in the essence of his teachings."

"Then you should go through the Tripitaka, which contains all his teachings. I can see you already have Dhammapada, a small but interesting treatise of his teachings. I hope you have gone through it."

"Not completely. But I have read many analytical books on Buddhism with different interpretations of his teachings by great authors like..."

"But why do you need analysis by different ones when the originals and translations of the work of Tathagat are available? Or do you have doubts about your understanding? They are written in very simple language. Anand and Upali did great work during the first council. Always go for originals. Analysis and interpretations only confuse. Analysts put their own mind into the originals and destroy their sanctity."

I now enjoyed talking to this man. He seems to be well-informed and conversant in Buddhism. He had just talked about Upali. It could be a normal fact for a student of the ancient history of India that the first council of Buddhism was held just after the death of Gautam Buddha at Rajgriha or modern-day Rajgir, presided over by one of the eldest and chief disciples, Mahakashyap. It is said that all the Sutra or Sutta was collected and noted by monk Anand and monastic rules or Vinaya by monk Upali with the help of fellow monks. Both are available today in the forms of Sutta Pitaka and Vinaya Pitaka. Although their historicity is still debatable.

"Interpretations are required when you are writing a thesis. Even on the Four Noble Truths, hundreds of volumes have been written. I wonder even Gautam Buddha could have been confused about what he meant if he had encountered so much analysis," I said in a lighter mood.

Suddenly, the monk started laughing out loud. Oh, the room was locked from the inside, or it would have drawn the attention of my mother or even my father if he had returned from the office. But nobody seemed interested in what was happening in my study.

It was interesting to see an age-old monk laughing. He could be in his late 80s or even early 90s, but he sounded very clear. He stopped laughing after 2-3 minutes.

"Dear sir, all confusion ceases to exist when one attains Nirvana. So, no question of Tathagat getting confused. For people, confusions arise when they mix their thoughts with what they hear or read. Tathagat's teaching is very simple, but people have become complicated. I wonder if the people who are trying to analyse are complicating things more and more."

"I understand your point, sir. Sometimes, people call his religion anti-God or anti-Soul. And there are different works, interpretations, and copies of the Tripitaka. There are even different schools like Mahayana, Theravada, Vajrayana, and everyone has different teachings. And there's Tantric Buddhism. Who will say what the original teachings of Buddha are?"

"Teachings are the same everywhere, but still, if you want to know what the originals are, better ask me. I will tell you what the originals are," the monk was smiling.

"Surely you will also be following some certain schools of Buddha, and you will also have a certain set of standards about his teachings..."

"No, Anand Kumar, the case with me is different..."

"Why, sir? Are you a direct follower of the Buddha who time-travelled from the past and joined me here to teach me the originals?" I told him rudely. Generally, I keep my calm during such discussions, but the monk was trying to dominate me with his 'I know all' style of talking. I have faced such opposition from many older elders. But still, he didn't mind my rudeness.

"Oh dear. Correct, you are, but only partially. Yes, I am a direct follower of Tathagat. But it is not time-travelling. I have been living for ages. I am the one who was present at the last rites of Tathagat when he attained Parinirvana. Born as Pippali, then Tathagat named me Kashyap, and later, I am called Mahakashyap. Therefore, you can also call me Mahakashyap," he told me.

I started staring at him. Do I look stupid? Or nonsensical? At least, that is what the monk was thinking about me.

Again, he smiled. Oh, how irritating his smile was. Surely, this monk was completely mad, and now he was driving me mad. Now, I am sure that I was discussing with a madman. Why am I tolerating a mad monk?

"Don't lose your temper, sir. If you are not agreeing with me, simply accept that you disagree. Tathagat always told his disciples never to give the key of your mind to another person. Isn't it, Anand Kumar?"

I had a sudden desire to react vehemently, but a sudden thought came to my mind, and I stopped myself from reacting.

"Never react aggressively, even if your opponent is saying something foolish," my guide always said. "It may be a bait by your opponent to make you weak. Always try to catch him off-guard. These are the basics of winning a discussion."

And my opponent was surely not a foolish one. I smiled.

"It feels nostalgic when you call me Anand Kumar. I've never been called by that name by anybody."

"Names are not important. You should know that you were known by some other name in a previous incarnation."

"Oh, really? But I don't remember either." Now I started playing his game. "Please tell me something more about my previous births. It will be interesting to know."

"Why don't I make you remember your previous births? It will be more interesting, and my work will become easier!"

I again felt that I was unable to control my irritation.

"Mr. Monk," I said in an aggressive tone, "You are a wandering person and always have lots of time to waste, but I do not. Please get to the point and let me do my study."

"Okay, sir. But if I prove here that I am the same person I am pretending to be, then what would be your reaction? Please answer this, and I will leave. Will you still ask me to leave?"

I started wondering. This thought had really come into my mind many times. If I could really go back in time and meet Buddha...

"But how is this possible, sir? Every fact about Mahakashyap that is available to me is also available to you. How will we, or I, cross-check them?" Suddenly, something came into my mind. Even discussing with this monk could be useful for my thesis. I said,

"Okay. Let it be. Just for the sake of discussion, now I am accepting for a while that you are the same person you are claiming."

"My pleasure," he smiled.

So, the discussion began. Discussions were going smoothly until he started spouting nonsense, quoting me as a person who was present during the time of Buddha in a previous life. According to him, the self-proclaimed Mahakashyap,

"Sir, I am not talking about Anand, the first cousin of Tathagat. I am talking about Anand Kumar now, the son of Sri Khaitan Kumar. It is another matter that he was known by some different name during the period of Tathagat."

4

So, Was It Fiction?

"So that's all, Bhaiyya? After that, you came out of the sleep?"

"No, dear. The story didn't end there." I expected such a response from Raj or from his sister.

"So?" There was a simple question mark on her face.

"After these revelations, there was some parting message by him: 'You have your own reasons to doubt me and not to believe me. Doubt is always okay, but to remain doubtful is not right. Better note down everything when I leave you and discuss it with like-minded people. I will join you tomorrow and will continue our discussion on the Four Noble Truths.'"

"Then your monk got up from your cot, moved towards the gate, and left, and you watched him go?"

"No, madam. I'm not sure about this." I said simply. "I'm really not sure."

"So what?" She really maintained her calm.

"It's true that after completing his parting message, he got up from the cot, but after that, I felt as if I had just come out of a deep slumber. I even thought that everything was a dream. A dream and nothing else. The room was still locked from the inside. I opened the door and asked my mum, still with her novel in the drawing room just outside my study, if anybody had come, and her answer was negative. My father was still late and hadn't arrived, as usual."

"And what about the time, Bhaiyya?" Raj was still enjoying the mystery.

"Even I calculated the time. I entered my flat at around six and entered my study after half past six. I would have fallen asleep after five or ten minutes. My eyes fell on him at twenty minutes past seven, and finally, I was out of slumber, or I may say that he departed at around eight."

"That means he was with you for at least forty minutes."

"You may say so. After asking my mother, I went back to my room, collected my memories, and wrote down all the discussions as he told me."

"Wow! Another locked room mystery! But without any murder," exclaimed Raj.

"So, AK, what next?" She was keeping her calm. She knew that I never discussed with her any nonsense. "I do know that you don't think I am going to believe this story as real. You would have something in mind when you are telling all these."

"Thanks, Ma'am," I said.

"For what?"

"For hearing me peacefully."

"Better say, reading it peacefully."

"Even I read it with great enthusiasm!" said Raj. I smiled.

"Thanks for the correction. I hadn't expected that you would read it with so much patience. I even thought that you would overreact, start laughing, or start scolding me for writing such a piece. But your composure, even after reading this unbalanced thing, surprises me."

"It depends, AK, it depends. The secret of my composure is that I knew that it had been written by the great Anand Kumar. You do know that I like your ability to reason."

Oh. I would have liked it more if she had told me that she likes me instead of saying that she likes my ability blah blah blah. Hope she will tell me some other day. But here she continues,

"So, tell me what you expect from me. Oh, forgive me. You just told us that your monk told you that he would be back the next day. So, you are expecting him again today! Then what are you doing here? It is already seven."

"My dear respected guide, please read my second draft again. I had mentioned that my monk, the respected one, came to me first on Wednesday. And by chance, today is Friday."

"Wow, Bhaiyya, do you want to say that the monk already paid a second visit to your study!"

"Yes, my lord!" I said dramatically, bowing my head with an eye on my guide. At the same time, he arrived and was present on the same cot, sitting cross-legged, staring at me with full compassion.

"Before you start, I want to discuss something."

I glanced at her with a question mark in my eye.

"I know that you are a no-nonsense person. Even you are a good manipulator of situations. You could explain a situation or relationship sometimes better than I could. You could have told me everything instead of passing me neatly drafted scripts. Still, I am accepting for a while that it was not a work of fiction."

"As Bhaiyya mentioned, he accepted that the monk is a real Mahakashyap."

"Exactly. Now, isn't it possible that the character of Mahakashyap has so engrossed your mind that you are feeling his presence as your other self? Even you have told me two or three times that you are fascinated by this character even more than Buddha. I think you would have read all the articles related to this monk available to you online and offline."

"You mean that a part of my mind is playing the role of Mahakashyap without my knowledge? Yeah, this could be true. Sometimes such things happen," I said with all the innocence.

"Just like chemical locha in the movie 'Lage Raho Munna Bhai'! When Munna Bhai started seeing Mahatma Gandhi!" exclaimed Raju.

"Yeah, something like that," she looked at me with bewilderment. Maybe she was expecting that I would oppose her theory. "So, you think that it could be true?"

"Why not? After all, how could one be alive for 2500 years? But how could I know what is real?"

"But it's so simple, Bhai. Just place a camera or CCTV in your room and record everything when he arrives next time."

"Even I was thinking about that. On Wednesday evening, everything was so shocking that nothing came to my mind. After the evening events, I was almost sure that everything was a sheer dream and nothing else. I never expected that he would come again. But he comes and promises to come again."

"Means you have an opportunity to make a recording."

"Yes, I have, but it may not work. Read my third piece of the draft and you can understand! But before that, tell me about the person who came across Buddha when he came out of 49 days of seclusion."

"Are you testing me? Everything is available about Upaka online and offline as a part of Majhim Nikaya."

"But I really don't know. It never came into my mind. Even my subject is related to the political drama of that period. I only know that Gautam went directly to his five friends after coming out of 49 days of silence at Bodhgaya and finding that his earlier teachers are not alive."

"But nothing more is available about him who belonged to the Ajivak sect. He met Gautam on the outskirts of Gaya, there were some interactions between them, and then he left. After that, he got married, bore a son, and met Buddha in subsequent incarnations. So many stories with variations are there. Even it is told that Buddha had to go to Isipatana, or modern-day Sarnath, by Akashmarg or through the air, but he changed his plan because he had to meet Upaka on the way!"

"Oh, so emotional! Gautam the Buddha changed his plan just to meet me!"

"But, Bhai, I have one more story about him. After 2500 years, he came again as Anand Kumar," Raj was always ready with interesting inputs.

"I understand that Upaka is not related to your work. But even Mahakashyap is not your subject. But your interests are there. Maybe out of love. Isn't it, AK?" She was smiling, biting her lips.

Oh, I always like the word 'love' from her mouth.

"Before reading about Mahakashyap, Buddha was my love, but he never came. But I started reading about Mahakashyap, and he started visiting," I said with a sigh.

"One thing, Bhai. I have visited your flat. It is also possible to open your room even when it is locked from inside."

Raj was not wrong. It was possible to open my room with the help of a key even when it was locked from inside as the lock was of a mechanical type. The spare key was always with my mother, but that was rarely used.

"You have a point, dear. So, it happens that somebody opened the door from outside to make way for the monk and later opened the door when his job was over. Probably done by my mother. Intelligent thinking. So, my mother is playing a game with me," the boy grinned.

"So, here comes the second probability. An interesting explanation by our Raju. Really, you have a good deductive mind. Even Aunty has good connections with monks. She told me last time that she visited the Ramakrishna Mission regularly and has a good rapport with monks. Maybe she has some connections with Buddhists. Even Bodhgaya is not far away from here."

"But why would she do such things?"

"Just to help you without letting you know. After all, she is not a simple lady. A good reader and a nice part-time writer she is."

She was not wrong.

"OK, I am also accepting this probability. Any prospect of a third one?"

"Yes. You are playing with our minds."

"For what?" I asked.

"Just to deduce something. Just to want to know our reaction."

"But why are you escaping the most obvious one?"

She stares at me with utmost seriousness.

"What, AK? That Mahakashyap really paid a visit to you? And you want me to believe this?"

"How dare I," I said, putting my hand on my chest. "I am just ticking all options, madam."

"Yeah," she said with a smile. "This could also be a decent option. Mahakashyap was in search of a new incarnation of Upaka for reasons and found him in Flat No. 105, paid a visit without knocking or opening the door of his room, and then slipped away after discussions."

"Now you are mocking me. But I know that this is not a rational probability."

"But I am not striking out even this option. Anything else, Raj?"

"But, Didi, tell me first, who was this Mahakashyap? I have heard about Siddhartha Gautama, his mother, and Mausi, and father. Even I have heard about his villain brother Devdutt and Sujata, and about his attendant Anand. But who was this old fellow?"

"Better ask Anand Kumar. At least he knows about him better than I do now, with some first-hand knowledge," she said.

I accepted her sarcastic remark decently by bowing my head.

"He was a Buddha at the time of Buddha."

"Don't confuse me, Bhai. Earlier you were telling me that he was a mere disciple of Gautama."

"Yes, he was. But it is mentioned that Gautam Buddha considered him at par with himself. Only he had the privilege of exchanging the chiwar with him. Also, it is mentioned that he performed the last rites of him."

"And it is also mentioned that he was completing his 120th year at the demise of Buddha and even lived for some more years," added Deepa.

"Isn't that too much, Didi?"

"Don't say it's too much, Bhai. In the Mahabharata, most of the characters fighting were in their late 80s or 90s. And don't count Bhishma Pitamah. He would have crossed

120 or 150. And mind it, if he really visited Anand Kumar, he would have crossed 2500 years."

I started blinking my eyes.

"And do all you history readers really believe such stuff? I mean, the Mahabharata or living so long?"

"It's a matter for another debate, dear Raj Kamal," I continued, "But facts go that not only he, even his wife, was a great adept."

"If both were great adepts, then what were they doing inside their marriage?"

"Answer, AK," there was a naughty smile on her face. "Tell my brother what both adepts were doing in a marriage contract."

"Search on Google and you will find the answer. Interesting stories are there. But later both got separated, and our monk joined Gautam the Buddha and soon attained Nirvana and became an Arhat."

"And his wife? What happens to her?"

"That would be part of another story, Bhai. But here, I am interested to hear part II of the story of the second day. Please continue, AK. We are eager to hear. Will you tell, or again will you make me read another script... oh, I can see there are more papers in your folder. I can see you are holding some more scripts."

I smiled and brought another sheet of paper with handwritten scripts on it and forwarded it to her. Raj also leaned in to read. He was more interested.

5

A Buddha in the Study Part II

"So 'dukkha', not sorrow, is the first noble truth, the first 'aryasachha'."

"Yeah. But you can use the word 'sorrow' in English or 'dukha' in Hindi as we have no parallel word in English or Hindi."

"But all the dictionaries agree with the translation; why not Buddha? When there is no happiness, there is sorrow. The absence of sorrow is happiness. The absence of happiness is sorrow. Isn't it?"

"No." There was a big no in his voice.

"But it is, sir. Talking about the second noble truth, he talked about the arising of dukkha or the cause of suffering."

"Dukkha Samudaya! Because there is only dukkha!"

"So, there is only dukkha, according to Buddha."

"No need to say 'according to Tathagat'. If it is a reality, then it is a universal truth. If something is not real, it is not, whether it is told by anybody."

"Even if told by Buddha!"

"Yes. Even if told by Buddha or Maitreya."

"Maitreya's word always confused me. But how could you talk about Buddha like that? After all, he was your guru!"

"He was and he is my guru. And he tells something because it is the truth. Not something that becomes truth because it is told by him."

"And who is Maitreya, about whom you just spoke? Even it is written in many places about him!"

"Oh really! Even you all can write about a person who is not even born!"

"Isn't it easy to explain a person who is going to be born in the future! You can fantasise about anything!" I giggled.

"Yes. Easier in comparison to a person who is history." At least there was something on which we agreed.

"Even you were fantasising about him when you talked about him."

"I am not, Anand Kumar. Because I happen to be the future guardian of Maitreya."

First, I thought to oppose his statement but changed my mind. After all, he is Mahakashyap! He is entitled to such statements!

"Then you are also entitled to know when he will arrive. Even so many people or gurus are claiming that they are Maitreya or the tenth avatar?"

"Now you are mixing two different stories of Maitreya and Kalki Avatar. Just like Tathagat is incorporated into the Dashavatara concept."

"Oh, sorry, sir. I don't know why I have similar feelings for Maitreya and Kalki Avatar. But I can see that even you have good knowledge about Hinduism and the concept of Avatar, embodiments of Lord Vishnu. Even you are good in English."

"I was made to learn, sir. It has already been more than twenty years since I came out of long Yoga-Nidra. Then, some other monks asked me to learn modern languages so that I could communicate and discuss with modern people. Even I was asked to learn some modern subjects. The funniest thing I came across was when I was told that Tathagat is now considered the ninth Incarnation of Vishnu."

"But what is the funny part of it, sir?"

"Sorry, Anand Kumar. I can see that the Hindu inside you has some reservations about my statement."

He was correct. But I could also see that he was not sorry for what he said. After all, Mahakashyap was famous for his adamant behaviour. I also noticed that for the first time he mentioned something about his new life of return.

"So, it has already been so many years since your return. Surely, you would have found a good place of solitude."

"Yes, sir. Shambhala has always been a great place for a person like me," he said with a smile. "Oh, I can see the sudden glow on your face when I pronounced the word Shambhala! Isn't it the most fantasised place on earth, dreamt of by all the seekers and mystery lovers? I am told that many people have tried to visit there, and many have claimed to have visited that place since the time Tathagat met the king of Shambhala. But during my stay, I found very few people able to reach Shambhala."

He was very truthful about Shambhala, also known as Gyanganj, simply the most fascinating place as imagined, but without valid proof. So much has been written about it as a place that could not be accessed by any physical means. Only a pure and highly elevated soul can access that place. There are persons who claim to have gone and stayed at that place to study higher vidya but without any documented proof!

"Yes, I can see that you are now travelling in the mental world of Shambhala. But it is not a place of imagination, so don't imagine it."

"So, it is a real physical place, sir?" I was still unable to accept that the person in front of me was from Shambhala.

"I don't know what your definition of physical is. But for me, it is a real place, as real as the place where I am presently sitting. But for you, it will be just a place of imagination."

"Put a CCTV there, and it will be a reality for everyone," I told him bluntly.

"And there will be another world with all the chaos of your regular world," his reply was equally blunt. "Therefore, there are places which have secured themselves from negativity. And there are also persons who can secure their presence and are approachable only by humans, and only when they choose to be exposed."

"You want to say that if I try to record you by any means, I will not succeed!"

"Yes, sir, I am telling the same."

"But you say that Shambhala exists within the geographical realm of this world and is still not approachable by our means."

"Yes, sir. But anybody can visit there, even you can, after fulfilling the requirements."

I kept mum. I didn't feel the need to ask what the requirements were.

"And what is the Kalachakra tradition? You mentioned that the day before."

"You already told the meaning by using the word. It is Kala Chakra, the wheel of time. The mystery of time is revealed here. Or you can say the original Big Bang theory is here."

The monk had a ready reckoner reply for each query. The expected discussion had been converted into a question-and-answer session. I continued my curiosity.

"Dalai Lama conducted a Kalachakra initiation some years before in Bodhgaya. What was that?"

"Better ask him. After all, he has been conducting the Kalachakra initiations all these years."

"But that was limited to his monks."

"Then join his lineage if you are eager to know that. You can't know everything from the outside."

"So, all the monks who completed the initiations of Kalachakra will know the mystery of time?"

"Ask Tenzin Gyatso, the present Dalai Lama. It is true that I was present at the time of the initiations at his request, but I was not a part of it. I hope he will spare some time to enlighten you. Still, you should know that many students sit for exams, but not all qualify."

The monk was sending bouncer after bouncer at me, and now I even stopped attempting to defend.

"I think you have already qualified that exam. It is written that you attained Nirvana within nine days of meeting Buddha."

"Yes. I am a good learner. But all practices like Vipassana and Kalachakra are for slow learners. If one is following mindfulness, no practices are necessary."

I fell silent without agreeing with him. It was better to continue our discussion.

"So, there is only dukkha. No sukkha or happiness."

"There is sukkha or happiness, sir, there is. But only as an extension of dukkha. Sukkha is always within the periphery of time."

"Yes, I agree. Both are time-bound, whether it is sukkha or dukkha. But everything known is within the periphery of time. Whether it is Janma or Maran, birth or death, to meet and to separate. And within the periphery of time, there is life."

"Oh dear, how beautifully explained by you! Everything known is within the periphery of time! Birth and death, to meet and to separate, all are limited by time. You told it, and you said it, sir!" Was he praising me?

I don't know why he suddenly became so happy. At least he didn't start dancing!

"That is what Tathagat meant when he said life is dukkha!"

"But isn't that a pessimistic approach to life?"

"Never, sir. When you say fire burns, it is a fact, not a pessimistic approach but a realistic one. Could you say that I believe in an optimistic approach to life and put your hand into the fire? Ha ha ha!" He started laughing at his own joke. "When you say that life is full of sorrow, it is a fact, not an approach, pessimistic or optimistic!"

"So, sir, you say that the world is dukkha, or full of sorrow, and this is because it is time-bound!"

"But you don't agree!"

"OK, I agree…"

"Oh, then simply say the world is full of sorrow, why 'if' and 'but' or 'because'?"

"OK, the world is full of dukkha!"

"And this is the first Arya Satya, the first noble truth. Agree?"

"Yes, now I agree."

"And this truth prevails for all seasons. It was an Arya Satta thousands of years ago, and it still holds good even now."

"Yes, sir. I accept this and bow my head to Gautam Buddha for revealing this."

"I am happy that I made you understand this. If every person could understand this and then the world will be free from chaos. Could we now start discussing the other three?"

"Surely not, sir," I told him with a confident smile.

There was a rare confusion displayed on his forehead!

"You want more clarification on it?"

"No, sir, now that is also a fact for me, the first noble truth. But I have some reservations about this observation."

"Please clarify, sir, I will be happy to hear your reservations and observations," said the monk with his usual calmness.

"Pardon me, sir, but thousands of years have already passed since Lord Buddha passed his sermon. And this is the twenty-first century. Do you still think his words hold good for modern people? Yeah, I accept that the world is full of sorrow, and there are ways out of it. So what, sir? A boy is preparing for exams, and he comes to know that the world is full of miseries. A man is supporting his family, and it is revealed to him that his world is full of miseries. Siddhartha Gautam had his rich parents to support his family. Do you think, sir, a person can balance his life, manage his worldly duties, and follow the path of redemption?"

He smiled, "Do you think, Anand Kumar, that religion demands an escape from family duties?"

"I am not saying this, sir. Please try to see from the perspective of a common man. A normal person, with all the responsibilities upon him, comes to know by heart about the Four Noble Truths. Could he still be able to perform his duties? Or will he start on a spiritual path?"

The monk closed his eyes for a while as if contemplating deeply on my queries. He opened his mouth and eyes simultaneously.

"You are trying to limit Gautam Buddha within these Four Noble Truths. Even the Dhammapada alone has more than 400 verses, which is only a very small part of the total treatise of the Tripitaka. Here we were discussing the Four Noble Truths, meant specifically for highly elevated souls. Every layman or a student of history cannot grasp the essence of the Four Noble Truths. These are not just statements; only a monk with a monastic life can receive the true spirit of them through the ashtanga marg."

"Then why were we discussing the Four Noble Truths or dukkha and sukkha all this time?" I asked, full of astonishment.

"Just to conclude that everything you know is within the periphery of time," the monk said with all the fanfare in his voice.

Although not satisfied with the reply of the monk, I said, "So, what is in the box for newcomers?"

"I think you already know about the Panchsheel, the five precepts for lay followers of Buddhism."

"Yes, I have heard about the five commitments proposed by Buddha for laymen. And I don't think there is any spirituality in it."

"Don't say that these commitments are for laymen. Laymen are those whose journey hasn't begun yet. These five rules are not as simple as they seem. They are the epitome of success in life."

"I don't get it, sir. These five rules were engraved thousands of years ago for contemporary people. Modern people are more complicated now."

"I have been observing people through all these years," said the monk with a beautiful smile, "and they are still the same, with chattering and gossiping minds. Hatred, grudge, selfishness, and fighting with different mental disorders within themselves. Only the subjects have changed. States and countries are still fighting for borders and waters. But there are always possibilities for change within oneself. Follow the Panchsheel, and you will start changing."

I was listening attentively. I don't know who this person was in reality, but I was really impressed with him now. I read somewhere that there was some dispute over the water of the Rohini River at the time of Buddha, which caused him to leave his home. And still, many states in India and other countries are fighting over water! A flash of thought came into my mind about discussing these political reasons for Buddha's departure, but I didn't think it proper. I continued the discussion,

"But what type of change, sir?"

"Change for the better," his reply was equally brief.

"If a man and his wife, with all the disputes within their relationship, start following Panchsheel, will he be benefitted?"

"Yes."

"So, if a student in his young age starts following Panchsheel, he will be benefitted in his studies?"

"Sure."

"And if an ailing person starts following Panchsheel, will he also get benefitted?"

"Death and ailments are for sure. But that one will live with peace even with ailments."

I was lost in thought for a while.

"Although I have read those five rules many a time, could you please repeat the Panchsheel for me?"

He smiled.

"Although those words were told by Tathagat in Pali, I read a translation of the same in English at the birthplace of him. I would love to repeat them." Then he told the same paraphrases I had read many times, but it seemed to me that I was hearing them for the first time,

"I observe, refraining from killing any living beings."

"I observe, refraining from taking what the owner does not give."

"I observe, refraining from committing sexual misconduct."

"I observe, refraining from telling lies."

"I observe, refraining from taking any intoxicant or drug."

"So, Panchsheel and the Four Noble Truths are all about Buddhism. But where do Vipassana and Buddhist meditation stand among all these? I have heard that you attain Nirvana through the practice of Right Mindfulness!"

"You mean Satipathana," his face was full of smiles. "It has all the essence of Buddhism."

"I have read about it, but I swear I understand nothing about it. Please enlighten me about it."

"Sure, sir."

Now, the monk was ready to reveal the unrevealed.

6

The Story Shared

"What are you thinking, Raju? I think Mahakashyap is also capturing your mind! Don't overthink, Bhai, otherwise he will also start capturing your study!"

"Didi! That would be great fun! I've been thinking about such adventures for all these years! Please WhatsApp me the Mahakashyap story, too."

"But what will you do? AK has cautioned us not to share them with anyone."

"I'll read it again and again and try to decode it."

Deepa asked Anand for a PDF copy of his story, and he happily forwarded it to her WhatsApp.

"Decode it! You mean you think there are mysteries behind it."

"You don't think so? Bhai was ready with everything. And he pushes everything step by step. Even he has a PDF ready with him. And how well he drafted everything. What do you think about it? Is it a framed one, or did such things really happen to him?"

"And what about someone putting the monk into his room? What an adventurous angle, Bhai! I think you have really included Agatha Christie in your syllabus."

"Is it impossible? Think about his mother as a mastermind lady. Just think of her as the latest version of Miss Marple, the evergreen old lady from the books of Agatha Christie. She masterminded a plot and allowed the monk to enter the room of Mr. Anand Kumar, our dashing hero, to captivate his mind with her engrossing stories!" His face was blinking like he had just solved some murder mystery!

"Oh, great, dear Holmes. And now you are going to reveal the reason for this crime. Because there should be a reason for such a crime. Some property involved and for that, it is necessary to declare him mad or so?"

"Elementary, dear lady Watson! She wants to outsmart him or wants to show her prowess. Or just a minute, the better probability is that the monk is playing with the mind of Mother. She convinces her that he has come from the past and her son Anand Kumar is the incarnation of that boy Upkar..."

"Upaka, you mean!"

"Oh, yes, Didi. The same Upaka. And now the mother is convincing and has allowed the monk to enter the study so that he could convince our hero of that."

"And in both cases, the monk is allowed by the mother!"

"Try to understand, Didi, if the monk was present in the study with his conversations, only the mother has the privilege to allow him. Mother was sitting outside the study in the drawing room. Nobody could escape to the study without coming into her view. Either Anand Bhai is telling a lie, or the mother has allowed the monk into the room, or the monk entered the room through thin air."

She looked at him with disbelief, as such an explanation was not expected from a sixteen-year-old.

"Wow! I never expected such summation from you, dear. Great analysis done by you!"

"Thanks, Sister!" said Raj, bowing his head, "At last, my intelligence has been recognised!"

"Yes, sir, but now a bit from my intelligence. Without rejecting anything from your analysis, I would say that these possibilities are far-fetched. Your hero said that the monk seemed to come from the air, and after the discussion, he departed in the same way. Ak never said that the monk uses the door. Does the monk use hypnotisation for that?"

"So, what is your analysis, Didi? Are you discarding his draft?"

"Really, it is easy to discard his draft by saying everything is nonsense. But I have known him for years, and I know that he is a no-nonsense person. He has many academics and researchers in his circle. He always knew that I was not going to believe even a shred of the story. But he came to me first."

"Maybe because he is closer to you. Or he wants to impress you." The young boy told her, smiling.

"I know him well. He is friendly with most of them," said Deepa, ignoring his smile. She again starts reading the draft.

"How well it is knitted, just like a damn good script from a best-selling novel," Deepa mutters in a low tone as if talking to herself. "Seems like pages are removed from some novel. An interesting character who came out of slumber after

2500 years and, after travelling here and there, came to Anand to teach him the Four Noble Truths and Panchsheel and to inform him that he is the monk Upaka in his 2500-year-old incarnation. How rubbish!"

"So, you are not going to believe this story."

"Oh no, never. I don't know why I listened and heard him with so much patience!"

"Because you always liked listening to him. After all, he is a great speaker!"

"And you are always a great admirer of him, brother. But if you want to judge a book, don't always start reading, forgetting who the author is. Suppose for a while that Mahakashyap really came from his long slumber. Then he must have some information and details which are still hidden from the eyes of historians. Do you know what history is? These are the events of the past which are supported by written documents, available artefacts, ecological marks, and some oral traditions. I think you have already heard about the Indus Valley Civilisation. During the 19th century, Charles Mason would never think what he had written in his book would change the course of Indian history. But do you know how the discoveries by later archaeologists after 1919 changed history?"

"Yeah, I know. It only increases the burden of our syllabus."

She smiles.

"Yes. As a student of history, we are always ready to rewrite ourselves. We will never know the perfect picture of ancient events, but this Mahakashyap is just telling his biography from history books."

"So, you are not believing the story."

"Oh! You still have a doubt about that? Yeah, keeping a bit of scope for your theory, I am accepting this draft as fiction."

"So, you are now throwing these pages into the garbage?"

"Oh no, dear. Even I would want to forward this to some WhatsApp group of intellectuals!"

"But Didi, Bhai has asked not to share..."

"But I want to. AK wanted to see my reaction to this draft, and now I want to see the reaction of others." She was all smiling.

"So, you want to forward it as your script?"

"Oh no! Not at all! I am not going to take credit for this. After all, I am not Anand Kumar, alias Upaka. I will forward it as a script forwarded by someone called Anand Kumar, who claimed it as his real story."

"Think twice, Didi. Lest Bhai wouldn't fall into trouble. Buddhists may claim copyright violation as Buddha is their copyright!"

"I can see you are talking like an intellectual. What are you eating these days?"

"The same you are preparing, my dear sister! After all, who else will take care of my dining needs!"

Deepa looked at her brother lovingly. He was twenty years younger than her, yet the closest person in her life. To those who didn't know them well, they might assume Raj was her son. After officially separating from her husband four years ago for no major reasons, she never considered remarrying.

Yes, there was some domestic violence involved, but that wasn't the main reason for their separation. She had seen worse examples of domestic violence in her parental home. There were also minor extramarital affairs on both sides. Rajan was physical with Sayera, and she was very friendly with Jitendra, though not physically. However, these were not the reasons either. Both were successful in their respective fields. Her husband was a practising Chartered Accountant, and she was a Reader in history, both earning handsome salaries, so there was no professional rivalry. Yet, they fought on a regular basis.

They had a love marriage, or at least they both claimed there was love between them before they married. They were from different castes, met regularly for at least six months, adored each other, and even exchanged kisses and gifts. Then, they got married against the wishes of their parents. So, they could say it was a love marriage. The marriage was a small affair with some friends from both sides. Raju, her brother, joined her after the marriage without any objection from her husband.

And then they got bored with each other. Yes, now this could be the reason for their separation. Just a while ago, when her brother claimed that Siddhartha got bored and left his house, it was revealed that they, too, had grown bored with each other. They always claimed to each other that they were not made for each other. This was revealed within 4-5 months of their marriage, and they separated within 18 months of their marriage without an official divorce. Her husband left her official quarters immediately. Yes, he had been living there since their marriage.

Now Anand, her student in some sense, is her present unofficial boyfriend, and he is six years younger than her. But who cares? Even Rajan was six years older, she thinks.

Raj has been living with her for seven years and is not interested in returning to his paternal village, where their father lives with another brother of hers. He last visited when their mother breathed her last. She was obviously not expected there since her marriage and didn't even attempt to go.

Now she was happy with her job and with Raju, and Raju was happy with her.

And with Anand Kumar. She has no problem admitting that there is no platonic relationship between her and AK. Yes, she was physically attracted to him but had yet to become physical with him. She knew that AK was attracted to her and never missed a chance to show his attraction.

After all, she knew she was attractive, if not beautiful, even in her late thirties. And she was alone. If these are not sufficient reasons, her attitude towards him completed the circle.

Last week she had been at his Flat No. 105 with her brother. And she could easily guess that his mother would not have appreciated the way she looked at her son. Oh, that look was intentionally just to tease her. After all, even her brother used to tease her for how he looked at her.

She opened her WhatsApp chat box. Now, she was forwarding the PDF to some colleagues and history enthusiasts.

Later, she would come to regret this act.

7

A Journey to Bodhgaya

I'm Rajkamal Verma, or Rajkamal, or simply Raj. Sometimes Raju, for my sister. Sunday is always a holiday, and for me, it's time to catch an autorickshaw to Bodhgaya, the place where Siddhartha attained Nirvana. It's about a 30-minute ride from Gaya. My sister goes to Bodhgaya six days a week, and the seventh day is reserved for me. But don't be confused, she goes there because her university is situated in Bodhgaya.

In ancient times, the city was known as Uruvela, and now it is the most important place for Buddhists and for me. Bodhgaya is about 13 kilometres from the ancient Hindu city of Gaya, and Sarnath is also 13 kilometres from another ancient Hindu city, Banaras. Just a coincidence, it seems. But almost all Buddhists maintain a handsome 13 km distance from Hinduism, don't they? Lalip always told me that Buddhism is the only religion where all are treated as equals. He is always very critical of Hinduism. Although I don't agree with him on this point, I never tried to oppose him. For me, he is the largest source of information on

Buddhism, and he is the prime reason for my regular visits to Bodhgaya.

Oh no, I'm not a Buddhist or a follower. I think I am too young for that. I just like visiting here, becoming part of the multinational crowd, sitting at colourful temples developed by Buddhist countries, and taking in the glorious Bodhi tree. Although my knowledge about Buddha was limited until last year, you know now, I have very good information about Buddhism, thanks to Lalip. We are very good friends now, and he also thinks so. He is around thirty years old, a Buddhist monk, his name is Lalip, he has brilliant knowledge about his religion, he is a good speaker, and I am a brilliant listener. So, the friendship happened.

When Anand Bhai was discussing Mahakashyap with Didi, I once thought about expressing my expert opinion about him, all gained through Lalip, but later decided to express my ignorance about him. Does the opinion of a sixteen-year-old matter among two distinguished history specialists?

"Truth be told, it can't be a lie even if told by a rogue."

"But nobody will take it seriously, Lalip." Lalit is very senior to me, but he still wants to be called by his name, even by me.

"But I will, Raj," he told me. The reality is that I never indulge in any argument with him. I ask, and he answers.

Today, we chose to sit on the stairs at Muchalind Sarovar.

"Tathagat spent his sixth week here after attaining Nirvana. It is told that the Snake-King Muchalind kept him safe under his hood during the extensive rain."

I took a fresh look at the statue of Buddha in the middle of the lake, sheltered under the hood of the snake. Another depiction of a snake, apart from our Hindu mythology!

"I presume that wasn't a real snake as depicted in our Hindu mythology. Maybe a Naag-ruler, I suppose."

"Oh, your mythology!" He never missed a chance to mock our Hindu mythology.

"But there are stories of the demon Mara trying to disturb Lord Buddha's meditation, once you told me."

"Oh yes, but that all was symbolic." Generally, Lalip presents himself as a Theravadin to convince my scientific mind where Buddha is a human being.

I wanted to intervene with the fact that the same may be true for Hindu mythology, but later, I constrained myself. I didn't want to start an argument with him. I changed the topic,

"Yeah. Last week, we were sitting at Nigrodha, where Buddha spent his fifth week."

"Your generation is always interested in shortcuts. You mean the Ajaapala Nigrodha Tree. Still, I'm glad you remember. If you agree, next week we will spend our seventh week at the Rajyatana tree."

"As you wish, Lalip."

"All wishes to the Tathagat. I hope your sister will join us again someday."

It was only once when I came here with Didi, and we met Lalit and had some discussions. He used to say 'She is intelligent and has a sharp mind but is very egotistic about her knowledge. Ego doesn't lead us anywhere.' Although I didn't like him judging everyone, as I said, I never opposed him.

"Also, bring that man AK also. He is really a gem and a good listener. We had a good discussion last time he visited with your sister. He speaks very nicely about you."

It was news to me. Didi came here with Anand Bhai, and both never informed me. Was that visit a date? Did they just forget to inform me, or was it intentional? They know very well about my rapport with Lalip and sooner or later, I surely would have known about their visit. Didi always told me everything, and she skipped informing me about that visit. It wasn't a big thing, but I really didn't like it.

"Lalip, I want to share something with you," I said in a serious tone.

I swear it was not a pre-decided act, and I never thought of sharing that draft with anyone. Maybe it was a sudden desire to show that I also had some secrets to reveal. I had saved that draft on my mobile anonymously when Didi forwarded it. I still don't know what mindset compelled me to do so. I opened the PDF and handed my mobile to him.

"What is this? Some media gossip?"

"Nothing of the sort. I know you don't like such things," I told him. "Just a part of a short story written by a friend of mine."

"A Buddha in a study! Oh, I like this heading. But you know I don't like Buddha in a fictional story."

"This is a story about Mahakashyap meeting a young man called Anand."

"Oh, then it will be interesting. You know, serious discussions about him have been going on here for a few days now."

"For what?"

"I could tell you, but you know there are some secrets maintained. Only monks from the inner circle are allowed to discuss such things," he said, making his voice more secretive.

"Oh, so you also belong to the inner circle!" I didn't know what the inner circle was, but still, I showed my astonishment.

"Not yet, but my seniors promised me so. But first, let me read it. Then I will discuss it with you further."

He started reading the small pieces.

The reality is that I hadn't expected that any above-par experience could be shown by my friend. But as he read the words further and further, his mouth fell open with astonishment.

After completing it, he looked at me as if he had seen a ghost. His face was losing its colour within seconds.

"Oh, that was just a piece of fiction and nothing..." I tried to calm him, but all of a sudden, he grabbed my hand and started running, dragging me out!

8

The Confusion Begins

"What's happened, friend?" Raj had already repeated his question many times, but Lalip was holding his hands firmly, seemingly oblivious to everything around him. By now, he had inadvertently pushed past many tourists, but he was neither aware of it nor did he care. It seemed he had been struck with a revelation and didn't want to miss his moment. Until now, he had been treated as an ordinary monk, but his time may have come.

Raj had already tried to snatch his hand away but without success. Raj was a gym enthusiast, but Lalip's grasp was stronger. By now, Raj knew he had made some grave mistake by allowing him to read that material. But where was he leading him? Surely to some senior monk? His sister had already dismissed the story as nonsensical, but he had never seen his friend so agitated. He had never seen anybody so nervous! This was really a piece of fiction, a simple story of a person meeting the legendary Mahakashyap in his dream—a piece of imagination with some normal discussions on Buddhism. And the story was incomplete!

Lalip stopped only when they arrived at the gate of a large campus with buildings inside. 'No trespassing allowed / No entry without permission,' as was written on the board at the gate. Raj had come to this gate many times to say goodbye to Lalip but had never entered. He knew that there were some office buildings inside restricted to monks and officials of the Temple Management Committee. Lalip generally didn't discuss his work, but once he had mentioned that he was involved in postal work inside.

There was security at the gate. Soon, Lalip was speaking with someone on a walkie-talkie provided by the security.

Within half an hour, Raj found himself inside a guest room, sitting on a sofa with Lalip standing beside him. There were three other people in the room, all properly introduced to him. One was introduced as Bhikkhu Dayanand, a senior monk in proper ochre-coloured robes, and the second was another monk called Bhikkhu Saran, who had joined here as an invited guest from another place. The third was a lady in a civil uniform. Raj already knew this lady; she was Ananya Singh, the Superintendent of Police of the district and was known to his sister. But hopefully, he had never been introduced to her. Still, he felt relieved finding a familiar face among them.

Raju was now full of wonder! What was she doing here? And above all, what was he doing here among these dignitaries? Although he wasn't a coward, he now felt scared. What kind of trouble was he in? And maybe he had also trapped his sister and Anand Bhai. He could feel his legs trembling.

His mobile had been taken from him before he was allowed to enter the room, and the draft had surely been read by all of them.

"So, a Buddha is in the study!" Bhikkhu Saran commented.

Raj kept mum. He didn't know how to respond.

"Do you know what mistake you have made, Mr. Raj?" the lady in the civil dress asked.

"No," he replied.

"How dare you write such a fictional story about our great Monk Mahakashyap? After all, he is not a fictional character. This is a severe crime, you know?"

Oh, that was the problem! He felt somewhat relieved.

"But I didn't write it. Someone forwarded it, so..."

"Don't try to fool me, boy. I know today's generations. They are always interested in making supermen's stories using historical characters."

"But I swear, sir. You can..."

Suddenly, something struck his mind. The PDF was forwarded by his sister. Could his sister fall into trouble if they found out that the PDF was forwarded by her? He quickly changed his words,

"Actually, I found it somewhere on the internet. I liked it and therefore saved it on my mobile."

"Still, the boy has committed a crime. Isn't that right, madam?"

"Yes, sir. And if there is a crime, there should be a punishment."

Suddenly, all three started laughing.

"Sorry, Raj, I think we scared you. There is nothing to worry about. He confused your story with something else and correlated it with some other things. We were discussing something else with our friends here this morning. Some words fell into his ear, and after reading your story, he thought that it was a plot, which made you run all the way here. I think Lalip has ruined your Sunday," the lady said soothingly.

Raj felt as if he had just been transported from a desert to the Himalayas. He looked at Lalip with reproachful eyes, who had already bowed his head, perhaps already feeling guilty.

"May I take some water?" Raj asked quietly, looking at the glass of water on the centre table.

"Why not, dear. Better yet, I will order some refreshments for you. After all, we all are culprits for making you afraid. Lalip, why don't you wait outside and allow us to calm this boy down? Otherwise I'm afraid he might start beating you for all your nonsense!" Bhikkhu Dayanand said.

All started laughing again. Lalip really moved towards the door.

Lalip is a very devoted monk. Forgive him for his mistakes. He has talked about you and your interest in our religion several times, and even mentioned that you wanted to visit here. But, after all, there are some protocols, and we can't allow outsiders here easily. You know there were some blasts outside a few years ago, and now security is very tight here. And there are also international threats, you know."

"Yes, sir, China is always ready to intervene."

"Yes, young man. Still, we believe in Ahimsa as we are followers of Buddha. There are always peaceful ways, but we should be careful about our people."

"Yes, sir."

"Oh, don't call me sir. We are monks, and you can call me Bhikkhu Dayanand."

"But I am very young, sir." Raj was very impressed by their openness.

"That doesn't matter, Raj. Every person has the capability to become an Arhat."

Raj had visited many temples and met many priests, but he had never heard such things from anyone.

"I am very impressed by you, sir—I mean Bhikkhu Dayanand. Please allow me some other time for blessings." He folded his hands.

"Sure, son. And here are some refreshments for you," the Bhikkhu said as a young monk entered the room holding a large plate. Raj had always wanted to know what they ate.

Before starting to eat, Raj turned to the SP, who was still holding his mobile,

"May I use my mobile now?"

"Sure, Raj." She handed his mobile back to him. He glanced at his phone, which was switched off. He remembered that the mobile was charged more than 80% when he first handed it over to Lalip. He also remembered that he had shared the unlock password with Lalip when he was reading the PDF and the phone had locked due to a timeout.

"Sorry, dear. I had switched off your mobile. You can switch it on now and proceed to your home as it is already 2 P.M."

Raj frantically tried to power on his mobile but to no avail. Didi might have been trying to contact him in the meantime. Now, standing outside the main gate, he fumbled with his phone, his attention only diverted when the sound of a bullet bike stopping nearby startled him.

He easily recognised the man on the bullet. It was Manoj Sharma, or Sharmaji, as affectionately called by his sister and him, a computer operator at his college and a regular visitor to their house.

"Madam has sent me; no more questions as it is an emergency. We must get away from this place as soon as possible."

"But why!" he exclaimed while climbing onto the bike. Today was full of unexpected events!

"You are in trouble. Actually, all three of you are in trouble!"

Suddenly, Raj sensed that everyone in the drawing room had been deceiving him. His mobile was intentionally damaged so that he couldn't contact his sister. They would have easily figured out through his WhatsApp that the PDF was sent by his sister. And who his sister was!

There surely was some mystery surrounding the PDF. And about the PDF creator, Mr. Anand Kumar!

"Hold on properly, Raj. Someone might be following us," Sharmaji warned as he accelerated the bike.

Raj turned his head and could see that two people were adjusting their bikes behind the large gates.

"No problem, Raju. I'm a champion biker, and I know every nook and corner of Bodhgaya."

"They could have traced the number plate of your bike through CCTV..."

"Surely, if it had one!" Sharmaji quipped with a sly grin.

Within seconds, his bike was soaring through the air, and within minutes, they had entered the nearby university campus.

Sitting behind him, Raju had the thrilling sensation that he was riding not with Sharmaji but with a spy!

9

The Problem Begins

A recently opened restaurant on the outskirts of the city, The Pearl restaurant soon became a centre of attraction for all South Indian food lovers. Although South Indian foods were not so popular in the city, The Pearl was still attracting lots of people. It was Sunday afternoon, and there was the usual rush in the restaurant. Anand and Deepa had already occupied a table and ordered two South Indian thalis.

"South Indian thali just for its name!"

"Don't say like this, madam. Taste the Rasam, and you will find pure Chennai taste."

"Everything is readymade. Open the pouch, add some hot water, and everything is ready with the so-called local taste of South India. If you want to know the real taste of Sambhar and Rasam, go to Chennai and taste it at any local restaurant."

"OK, madam, done," said Anand with all smiles. "Plan a South India tour and count me in. We will taste all South Indian foods."

"But why me?" she said, winking her eye, "I think you are old enough to travel anywhere alone."

"Oh no, madam. I am still afraid of travelling alone. I'm even scared of going to restaurants without any escort," Anand said, winking his eyes.

"Don't try to take unnecessary lead, Mister. I am your senior. Limit your thought to this so-called South Indian rice and rasam."

"I agree with you, Professor. It is true that Sambar should be spicier. But better to say that Sambar should not be part of such a thali. But the worst thing is that they are not using coconut oil. A South Indian thali without coconut oil! Really a shame!"

Both were looking at the person sitting at the nearby table with full surprise, who was interrupting them.

Without any formality, the stranger got up even before completing his sentence and dragged his chair to their table, comfortably adjusting himself on it.

"Don't overreact, Anand. I was hearing your conversation sitting there. But when you hadn't started anything relevant, I came here to interrupt you." Now he had settled his head at the back of the chair.

Anand wanted to say something bitter for disturbing them, but she stopped him with a gesture. She already guessed from his tone that the stranger was not an ordinary man.

A high-level criminal or some police officer? She said in a normal voice,

"I can see that you are well acquainted with us. You even addressed me as a professor. I am not one, but could be one within three or four years."

For a moment, there was a glimpse of disappointment in the eye of the stranger. Such a response from her was not expected! He could see how she calmed her partner.

On the other side, she was now more cautious. Her charm, her personality, and her skills as a speaker (if we count that), even in her late 30s, often attracted even the young ones. It was a small town, and she could easily guess her fan following. But since yesterday, she sensed some strange-looking people. If she guessed right, she was even followed during her morning walk. Although she was a popular figure here, such things were unusual!

"By the way, we are already impressed with your knowledge and if you have something else in your store to say or discuss, we would be happy to spare some time another day."

He smiled.

"I am impressed with your oratory skills, madam. But believe me, you have no other option except to tell me everything. You have a good reputation here, and we don't want to malign it."

"Oh, the man wants you to disclose something. Disclose it, madam. It is not proper to hide," Anand said in a jocular tone.

"But first, the gentleman should disclose what he wants to know," Deepa replied in the same tone.

"I think you are not taking me seriously, but the fault is mine," the stranger said calmly. "I should have disclosed my identity. I am Charan, but you can call me Charu. Although I am very reputed in my circle, for you, I am a senior field officer in some investigation department of the central government. You may call it CBI, RAW, or anything else, but as per the ID issued to me, I am an employee of the Cabinet Secretariat." He extended his ID card to her. "Generally, we don't show my identity to any layman like this Anand Kumar, but as you are a reputed lady, I beg to do that."

"Thanks for such honouring words. If this discussion is between two respected dignitaries, I should take my leave." It was another matter that he was not going to leave her in this situation. She was surely in danger.

"No, Anand Kumar. You are the main culprit for us and already in danger. It is just a matter of time before you will be in lock-up facing third-degree interrogation. Some policemen are already outside."

His fuse blew up in a moment! He couldn't even remember a simple fight with anyone. And Deepa was also involved. Did her ex-husband complain about their relationship? But what would a government detective have to do with this?

"Could you please tell me what the matter is?" Anand asked.

Charu smiled. He always liked the submissive tones.

"Thanks for asking. I have always believed that academics are law-abiding people. Initially, I was told that you both should be taken into custody before interrogation. But I declined. It would push the panic buttons. Wouldn't it, madam?"

She had understood by now that the situation was grim.

"Sir, if you don't mind, please join me at my residence. My car is parked outside, and it is only a ten-minute ride to my home."

"That will be nice, madam. Even my car is also outside, but I will pick mine later as I am joining you in your car."

After all, what was the problem with Charu not wanting her to be left alone for a while? She had led a clear-cut life until now. The better part was that her brother was away in Bodhgaya. It was already half past one, and he wouldn't return for at least two more hours, as per his usual Sunday routine.

"OK, let's depart. Clear your dues at the counter and join me outside."

Within ten minutes, they were at her destination where there were more surprises. Her quarters' gate was opened and seemed to be ransacked. Some persons in civil dress were already there.

"Sorry, madam. It escaped my mind to inform you that my team is conducting a search in your house without permission. You have the right to complain against us. But before further discussions, we should relax ourselves on the sofa. And my officers, you can also find some place to relax."

Both looked at each other. Whatever the matter was, both now knew it was time to use their contacts.

"May I make a call?"

"Oh sure, madam. Hope it will help you. It has been some time since you last called your brother. Hopefully, he will be returning from Bodhgaya."

"But I want to call one of my friends."

"Then let me guess her name... Oh, okay, I think you are going to call Ananya Singh, the city SP! And I can see your student is also trying to message somebody. No problem."

Gosh! This man had done all his homework properly. Anand looked at Charan with utmost surprise!

"I think I've upset you. Please call your friend, or just wait for some time. She texted me a while ago that she is busy talking to your brother at the TMC Office. She will surely call you after their discussion."

Anand could see the changing emotions on Deepa's face. After pressing some keys on her mobile, she placed the mobile on the table.

Only Anand noticed that she had texted somebody just before switching off the mobile. Had she asked for somebody's help? He had done the same.

"Now you can start asking questions," she said in a firm voice.

The first question itself cleared the air between them. Or did it make the matter more confusing?

"Where is MMK? Oh, sorry, Monk Mahakashyap, Mr. Anand?"

Both looked at each other with extreme surprise.

"Yeah, the same Mahakashyap who met you on Wednesday evening at 105. And don't tell me that you don't know him. You have already confessed, and your story has been with me since Saturday morning. I received it through some channel."

Anand looked at Deepa. Her face was now emotionless.

"Don't blame her, man. She forwarded it to her circle, and one of them forwarded it to another, and that person forwarded it to someone close to us. So simple."

"And my brother? Why is he held captive?"

"Oh, he is not held captive. Just some discussions have been had with him. We didn't want to involve the local police. But your brother showed that story to a monk at Bodhgaya, and the matter was unnecessarily disclosed. When I was informed, I was compelled to take SP Ananya Singh into confidence. But I am surprised that she hasn't submitted her report to me yet. You know these local cops!"

Suddenly, Deepa started laughing, looking towards Anand with full eyes.

"You are in trouble, AK. Now tell Mr. Charan about the whereabouts of MMK, I mean Mahakashyap. It is entirely your story. And Mr. Charu, the story is entirely his. Where do I come into this? Instead of going to his house, you are troubling me. Furthermore, you are even troubling my brother. Are you nuts? The monk visited his house on Wednesday and then again on Thursday, as he himself proclaimed. I only came to know about all that when he submitted the draft to me via WhatsApp. The same draft I forwarded to my younger brother Raj, who supposedly shared it with his friend in Bodhgaya. Am I right, AK?" Deepa said with all smiles. She had already made up her mind to stay away from this matter. After all, what was her fault? It was now certain that he was involved in some scheme, and she wanted to distance herself from all these.

"But madam, what about the monk staying here? After all, you are going to be his host."

"What!" Another new story! She felt like banging her head.

Suddenly, Anand interrupted loudly,

"Oh, madam. I think you haven't read my script properly. Mr. Charan is probably referring to the postscript I wrote in which the monk said that he wanted to spend this weekend at your home."

Only now did she understand her involvement in the case. AK had forwarded her an extended version of the draft, and she hadn't had time to read it again. So, the same extended version had been forwarded by her to her friends!

"I will kill you," she said in a cold voice. She would have surely slapped him had it been some other time.

"I think your personal discussion is over. Now inform me, where is the monk? And if you have even the slightest intention of being non-cooperative, I have some better ways to extract information from you both."

"OK, sir. I will tell you. But first, inform me, who is this Mahakashyap?"

Charan got up and delivered a tight slap to Anand's face, then returned to his place. Blood started dripping from his lips.

"Let me repeat the question. Where is Mahakashyap?"

This was the moment when the SP's jeep entered the campus.

"These cops always arrive at the wrong time," Charan murmured, then shouted,

"Come in, madam. I was waiting for you. I see you brought a monk. Where is the boy?"

"He escaped. Actually, there was no need to hold him for long."

10

The Problem Deepens

"So, you will teach me how to work? Do you know where I have come from? A single complaint from me could transfer you to the deadliest place, you know? First, you allowed that lad to escape, and now you're interfering with my work!" He was almost yelling, using every possible slang.

"I only know that you have entered the house of a respectable woman with some of your staff without any search warrant. You are spitting dirty words at a lady police officer on duty. You are manhandling a person without any guilt. I also received commands from my superiors to resolve the issue peacefully. First, try to convince them about the gravity of the situation. After all, you are not dealing with Pakistani terrorists. Here, Mr. Saran is also with us for help."

So, she had messaged her friend Ananya Singh!

It lasted for almost ten minutes. Now, at the end, only five people were left in the room. Knowing the identity of Mr. Saran, he decided to cool his nerves.

"I must accept that this is one of the first cases where I have had to work with limited resources and without much fanfare. After receiving the story from Anand, I thought that we had solved the riddle. But now it has complicated the matter. If your story is really a work of fiction, then its timing is remarkable. Just a week before, last Sunday, we started to search for the trail of this MMK, and within three days, on Wednesday, Anand disclosed his meetings with him to madam Deepa. And now he is claiming that he is writing fiction."

"Sorry to interrupt, Mr. Charan, but what is MMK? At least address him as Mahakashyap or simply the monk," Saran said in his usual calming voice.

"Sorry, sir. It is not meant to demean him. But his name is so long, therefore our branch is using this code name, also for the sake of maintaining secrecy. But I will try to use the full name in front of you."

"Respect should come from within. So please continue as usual. And Anand Kumar, so, you never met the Monk Mahakashyap. Then how did the idea come to you to write about him? Our Mr. Charan has objected to the timing of your writing, so you have to clarify."

"Yes, that can be explained. I was at the university last Monday, and after my work, I went to Bodhgaya. Madam was also with me. Someone there mentioned that Mahakashyap is the guard of the future Buddha, and he will return one day. So, I started thinking about it. You know, I am writing a thesis on the same subject, and this character fascinated me the most. Thus, a story came into my mind about how he would interact with me if he paid a visit."

"And who is this someone, who discussed with you at Bodhgaya?"

"His name is Lalip, and he is also a friend of Raju."

"Yeah, I know him," Saran said.

"And what about the phrase you wrote that he wanted to stay at this house?"

"That is just to make my fiction more real," he said with a shy smile. "You know that today is Sunday, and no monk is available here. You can even check the CCTV footage outside."

"Have you checked his home?" Saran asked.

"Yes, that has already been checked. His mother has cooperated well," Charan answered.

There was silence for some time. Deepa broke the silence,

"May I ask a question?"

"Sure."

"What AK, I mean Anand, has written is about a monk who lived around 2500 years ago. And if I am not wrong, you are searching for a person whose name is also Mahakashyap and who is a Buddhist monk, surely a person from this age. Then why are you all intermixing both stories?"

Charan looked at Saran, expecting a better answer.

"Please enlighten us, Bhikkhu Saran. Even I want to know this."

"Because the monk we are searching for claims to be the same Mahakashyap, who lived at the time of Tathagat, probably in a new body," he answered simply.

"The same stupid story again," Charan murmured.

"Don't need to say so quietly, dear sir. I am all ears."

"Then please say things that could be easily accepted by all."

"I said that he claims such a thing. I am only mentioning his words."

"Then please explain how it all starts if it is not abided by any protocols," Anand said.

"No problem, sir. You already mentioned most of the things in your story, and the rest—historical details—are already available online or through published books. But let me introduce myself," Saran said. "Saran is my pet name. I am a Kalon, dealing with security matters of the Tibetan Government-in-exile."

"I am told that you are equivalent to a defence minister of your state. I hope you mean the same."

Anand raised his eyes and looked at Deepa with astonishment. They were now dealing with a minister of a government. Deepa had once visited McLeod Ganj, the centre of the Tibetan Government in India. Now, they could understand the reason for Charan's changing tone when Saran entered the room.

"Yes, sir. We are searching for one of our monks, Mahakashyap, who left our settlement three months ago to visit Bodhgaya. He visited here with some other monks. All other monks returned to our settlement well within time, but Mahakashyap informed them that he wanted to return after visiting some nearby Buddhist places. He was well within our contact, but suddenly, he stopped contacting us about twenty days ago. We tried to locate him through our friends at Bodhgaya but without any success. As he was one of the most important figures among us, we had no other option but to contact our counterpart in Delhi."

"You mean our government ..." Charan didn't like comparing their government to his. That small group was comparing themselves with them!

"Yes sir. And we really feel honoured that your esteemed government took immediate action and put their machinery to work."

"Our government always believes in benevolence," Charan added.

"But I don't understand one thing. Why is this monk so important to you? And who would be interested in harming a mere monk?" This time, Ananya interrupted.

"Our group is very small, madam, and everyone is very important to us. It is always our duty to protect each and every one of our citizens."

"If I am correct, there have been cases of missing monks before. But it was the first time that our defence machinery was contacted."

"Yes sir. But he is one of the most learned monks among us. He is versed in English, Hindi, Tibetan, and even Chinese. He can explain all our scriptures with ease. And it was also the first time that one of our monks informed us that some Chinese persons attempted to kidnap him."

Charan kept mum for some time. Even his team was informed that some Chinese spies had been seen at Bodhgaya. He was also informed that this MMK had sent such a message to his friends before disappearing. He felt irritated. Due to these Tibetans, they were always getting into tensions with the Chinese. Ananya intervened in the conversation this time,

"So that is the issue. But enlighten me further. Deepa and Anand just said that there are discussions in Bodhgaya that historical Mahakashyap is going to return," Ananya Singh asked.

"You mean he will time travel? Oh, this is more interesting!" Charan laughed mockingly. "What do you have to say, sir, about this? Isn't it like saying that the old-time Mahakashyap and this missing Mahakashyap are the same? Oh, that will be real fun! Please enlighten me also. I have heard that you people are experts in enlightening anybody!"

"Nobody can enlighten anybody, sir," Saran smiled, "and how could I say that both are the same? Only Mahakashyap can confirm such things. Please ask him when you meet him."

"And what is the Chinese connection, sir?"

"Tibetan people have always had some problems with China."

"Or vice versa, if you allow me to say so," Saran added. Charan didn't like the interruption. He added,

"I don't know if the respected minister knows this fact or not, but there is a perception among his people that this Mahakashyap is the same one who lived thousands of years ago," Charan revealed bluntly.

Saran didn't like this revelation among all present but didn't reveal this on his face.

"Everybody has the right to form an opinion, I suppose. Anand Kumar also opines something in his story. Even he has the opinion that he is the incarnation of someone."

"And what does your MMK, I mean, the monk, think about himself? A simple grand old monk or a thousand-year-old one?"

"As I said, sir, please ask him when you meet him. I am very positive about your intelligence skills."

He looked at Saran. Was he showing his belief in him or challenging him? He shook his head, clearing his mind. His present target was to catch that MMK anyhow and hand him over to his superiors without intimating these Tibetans. He knew that there was also another security team on his trail.

The sound of an auto stopping outside disturbed them. Deepa opened the gate. It was already evening, and she was surprised to find Raju outside. He should have been with Sharmaji. She had texted him to pick up his brother. She looked at the watch. It was already seven in the evening.

Raju was initially stopped by Charan's men, but Charan allowed him inside.

"So, you are Raju who just fled from the Bodhgaya office."

"Not so, sir," he replied, surprised, "I was asked to go after the meetings. If you don't believe me, please confirm with SP Didi or Saran sir. They were also present there."

Charan turned his head to them.

"Yes. The boy is right. We allowed him to go after necessary interrogation. There was no point in keeping him there."

"But you said that he escaped."

"I didn't mean it that way. I just said that after the interrogation, he left us. Someone picked him up on his bike."

Charan kept staring at him.

"Actually, when I came outside, I met Sharma Uncle there, and therefore I took a ride."

"And who is this Sharma?"

"Mukesh Sharma. He is a computer operator working at my college. He is familiar to us."

"Hope you didn't message him to pick up the boy?"

"Never. How could I have known that Raju was there?"

He fell silent. She had played her cards well right under his nose.

"And Master Raju, I can see that you are not surprised to see us here. I think you were expecting us," he stated.

"You are right, uncle. The person who brought me here informed me all about you. He even told me that a senior field officer, Mr K V Charan from RAW, with five supporting staff, will be interrogating your sister and Anand Bhaiya in the presence of Saran and SP Didi."

His face turned red for a while.

"And who was the person who picked you up? The same Sharma?"

"No, sir. Sharma Uncle dropped me at the bus stop as he had some other work to do. I waited for half an hour there to catch a bus, but unfortunately, I didn't find one. Then I got a lift from someone."

Ananya interrupted, "We left you there before three P.M. And you are arriving here after at least four hours. So, it was a long journey for you. Also, I could guess now that you had recognised me as your sister's friend but didn't think it necessary to reveal. Intelligent boy you are."

"You also didn't reveal it either, Didi, and you also disturbed my mobile," Raju said, smiling. "And the travel time wasn't so long. The person who gave me a lift on his bike was really an interesting one. As I was not in a hurry, we took some rest on the way and had some good discussions. He was an interesting person with a profound knowledge of Buddhism. Although he was a bit old, he drove very well," Raju said excitedly.

"Oh really! Then we would also love to meet him. I hope you asked his name," Saran said.

"The interesting part was that his name was also Mahakashyap, but he was not dressed like a monk."

Everyone's face showed surprise, but Charan was the most startled. He almost jumped from his sofa, quickly pulling out his mobile and showing Raju a photo.

"Is this the same person?"

"Oh, yes, the same one who gave me the lift. So, you know him too!" Raju exclaimed excitedly.

"Give me the number of his bike," Charan shouted and started running outside.

"I'm not sure, but it was either 6742 or 6247... and it was a Rajdoot," he began.

Within seconds, Charan was outside, shouting orders to his men to initiate a chase. Ananya sprang into action, rapidly dialling numbers on her phone.

Now, the drawing room was left with only three occupants, as the Tibetan minister had also left with the SP.

Everyone heaved a sigh of relief.

"What a stormy day it's been!" Anand remarked.

"And it all started with a stupid story," Deepa responded.

"Not madam. It started when someone began forwarding it."

"Yeah, I accept my mistake. But how could I have known it would coincide with another story? But the real masterstroke was played by my brother, which drove out all the unwanted guests. And I can see you seem more energetic and enthusiastic even after a day-long journey. But first, give me a hug. I was more worried about you," she said, holding and hugging him affectionately.

"Oh, I can see you are a bit emotional, Didi," Raj said, hiding his emotions. "But what masterstroke are you talking about?" he asked, surprised.

"That Mahakashyap bluff. But how did you know the name of that detective? I didn't tell you that. I just messaged you that some detectives are here. Didn't this storyteller message you the details?"

"But everything I told you is true. I really met that old man, and he told me his name was Mahakashyap."

Both were now looking at him in surprise.

"So, you met Monk Mahakashyap, and he discussed Buddhism with you!" Deepa exclaimed, still finding it hard to believe that her brother had spent time with someone who was on RAW's search list.

"Yes. But what's the issue?"

Anand explained everything in detail.

"Did anyone notice you with the monk?"

"He left me at the colony chowk where some usual shops were open."

"I hope someone saw you with him. Otherwise, that detective might think you are lying. But first, tell me what you discussed."

"Sure, Didi. But how could he dare to slap Anand Bhaiya? I didn't like that part."

"He could have done worse. But the SP's entry, especially the minister's presence, spoiled his plan. But one thing I don't understand. How did that monk know about the police officers?"

"Maybe Mr. Saran informed him. After all, both were Buddhists," guessed Raju.

Everyone was lost in their own thoughts.

"But first, tell me about your meeting with the monk," Raju started his story.

11

A Journey With a Monk

"I've never seen an old man ride a bike with such ease. By the way, how old are you? I don't think you're any less than 70!" I remarked, eyeing the wrinkles on his face. He had a good physique for his age, but his height couldn't have been more than five foot seven or eight inches, I supposed.

"Maybe a bit more than that. I've lost count," he said with a usual smile. I started guessing his ethnicity. Surely, he wasn't Indian. Or was he from a north-eastern state? Or perhaps from China or Tibet? In Bodhgaya, you'll find lots of faces with such features.

"Don't get confused with so many guesses; I'm here to answer. I'm purely local and have been living in Gurpa for a long time."

I was really surprised to hear that he was local. Except for his dress, he seemed to be a Buddhist. Maybe he read my face well.

"Don't get confused by my dress. I am a Buddhist, an ardent follower of the teachings of Tathagat."

Is he a mind reader? Or is my face more transparent? Anand Bhai always said that my face is a perfect index of my mind.

I glanced at the bike. He had parked it a while ago near a tree, and we were taking a rest in an abandoned tea shop near the highway, sitting on a cement platform meant for customers.

I looked at him again. He was remarkably fair, and his face was full of wrinkles, without a single sign of hair on his face or head. I started to wonder what kind of shaving cream he used!

"I'm returning from Rajgir and am a bit tired. We'll continue our journey soon if you're not in a hurry and if your parents won't complain."

Eight more kilometres to Gaya. It was four o'clock, and I wasn't in a hurry. Sharma Uncle had told me not to return home before six. Didi had instructed him so. Still, I really failed to understand what was going on!

"Actually, the opposite is true. I'm told to return after six. Even if I reach before then, I'd have to wait somewhere in Gaya until six."

He laughs.

"Then why don't we stay here with me until six, and then we can continue our journey? I think this is a good place to take some rest."

I look around. We were sitting on a raised platform of an abandoned tea shop, which was properly shaded—a real respite from the heat outside. It was the first week of March, yet the temperature was soaring, as usual. When you live in Gaya, temperatures start rising even from February. I returned my gaze to the monk. He had introduced himself as Kashyap when I first met him at the tea shop near the bus stop. I wondered if Kashyap or Mahakashyap is a common name for a Buddhist monk. Initially, I had planned to reach Gaya and spend time at one of my friend's houses. But now, I found it better to spend some time with the old monk. Buddhists attract me, and today was a wonderful day with interactions with some esteemed Buddhists. But what was going on with Didi as she wants to keep me away from my house? Some usual stuff? First, she sent Sharmaji there. And how did she know that I was there?

"So, you were returning from Bodhgaya? A regular tour?"

"Yes, uncle. I come here every Sunday. You know, my sister visits daily, and Sunday is for me. I like the atmosphere here. One of the monks is my friend. His name is Lalip. I enjoy talking to him..."

You know, I'm not very talkative. Even I admit that I'm shy and have a very limited number of friends. It's tough for me to talk to strangers. However, when I met Kashyap Uncle, everything seemed easy. I even started the conversation with him, and now here I am, sitting with him, continuing to talk about myself. I could see he was listening to me attentively. I just felt like I was sitting with my grandfather, rambling on about unnecessary things. I paused for a moment.

"So, you live in Gurpa. It's a very small village, I think. I've heard about it. Sometimes tourists at Bodhgaya ask me about its location. I still don't know what it's famous for."

"Gurpa is famous for me. I live there." He started laughing. I joined him in laughter. His laughter was as sweet and innocent as a child's.

"Your sense of humour is very good, uncle."

"And you are a nice soul. Most come here with family or friends, but you come here to discuss with a monk. Even I could see that you have a mobile phone in your pocket, and you haven't used it for a while."

"Thanks, uncle. But there's another reason I'm not using it. It's damaged." I couldn't resist telling him about today's adventures.

He listened attentively and started laughing again when I finished my story.

"Interesting. So, they think that what your brother has written is his real experience and somebody is proclaiming that he is the real Mahakashyap! They must be nervous to imagine this." This time he laughs more loudly, and again I joined him.

"But I still can't understand the case. Even the SP was there, and they are investigating something. My sister informed me through her staff to remain outside for some more time. Then Anand Bhaiya has written some stuff and he is also in trouble, as Sharma Uncle told me briefly. I failed to understand anything. If Bhaiya's story is true, then why is someone pretending to be Monk Mahakashyap as a time traveller! Who will take this stupid idea seriously!"

"Really, so much doubt. Doubt is always good, but never accept it, dear."

"But what will I do? I am dying to know what is going on in my house. Why did my Didi ask me to come home late? Is she in trouble?"

"Why don't you ask someone to visit your house? Tell someone to visit your house and report to you."

"Even I am thinking of this. That's why I am missing my phone."

"Then why don't you use mine? I have one too." He never opens his mouth without smiling.

Oh! I should have guessed that a person with a bike would also have a cell phone. He took out his phone from his pocket, and it was an iPhone 14 Pro Max. Oh! I was expecting a keypad phone.

A monk with an iPhone! First, he extended his mobile to me then suddenly changed his mind.

"Better tell your address to me. I will send someone to your home, and he will check your house. You know, I have high-level contacts there."

An old monk driving a 350cc bike, using an iPhone latest model, and with high-level contacts in Gaya! I provided him my address and soon he was busy talking to his contact in English with a perfect accent!

"I was expecting a basic mobile."

"Because I am a monk? But you know, this is the safest model. Yes, I like technology. Use technology, but never allow technology to distract you. I noticed you've touched your pocket where your mobile is multiple times, even though you know it's switched off."

I thought about objecting, but restrained myself. He was absolutely right. It didn't seem right to start a meaningless argument with such a wise man.

"You are right, uncle. Many times, we unknowingly do things that we later regret. Anand Bhaiya told me to do Vipassana meditation to get rid of this habit, but it hasn't helped much. Maybe I'm not doing it correctly."

He started laughing again.

"Sorry, Raj. It's like using a sword to clean the dirt from your ear."

I looked at him in surprise, not understanding what he meant.

"Then what should we do?"

"First, start using the word 'I' instead of 'we'. It's your problem. Why involve the entire society in it? You should learn to shoulder your responsibility." It was the first time he seemed serious. I nodded, seeing no reason to disagree.

"Then learn to laugh at your own stupidity."

I looked at him again, as I didn't understand.

"It's simple, dear. Start laughing at your own stupidity. Whenever you realise your body is trying to invade your mind, start laughing at yourself. Suppose you are reading and get distracted by unnecessary thoughts, just start laughing! Oh! I see your hand just tried to touch your mobile again!"

And he started laughing. He was right, and I couldn't help but join in.

"Oh, and there it goes again, your finger struggling towards your pocket!"

It turned into a riot of laughter between us, and we almost fell to the ground, continuing for almost five minutes!

"Now you can see how simple it is! When you're aware of the absurdity of your actions, your mind will stop repeating them."

"But it's not that simple, Uncle," I said after a pause from our laughter. "I'm a student, and I can see how the mind always plays the spoiler. Whenever I start reading, my mind starts playing different videos, always swinging between past and present."

"That's because it's the mind, dear. That's its duty. Just stop fuelling it, and it will slow down automatically."

"And what fuels it?"

"Ah, think about it. Don't dwell on your past. Don't daydream about how you'll celebrate your good results. Oh, here's my contact calling me."

He was now taking the call. Soon, he ended the call and began updating me about my sister and the uninvited guests.

"So now there's nothing to worry about. We can proceed to Gaya."

He started to rise.

"But our conversation isn't over," I said, clearly disappointed. "Could we wait a little longer?"

"Sorry, dear. But I have more appointments," he replied, his smile returning.

"At least could you share your number?" I was really not ready to part with such a congenial person.

"Give me your number. I'll call you soon. I'm also interested in meeting your sister. I've heard she is quite profound in Buddhism."

So, my sister is so popular that even a monk is eager to meet her. I gave him my contact number.

"Please save it as Rajkamal or Raju."

"And I am Mahakashyap, but you can remember me as Kashyap also," he says, shaking my hand.

I am astounded! Another Mahakashyap!

First, there was the Mahakashyap who met Anand Bhaiya in his story, if that really was just fiction. Then, another Mahakashyap over whom Lalip became overly excited. And now a third one in front of me, sharing his wisdom.

"But you initially told me your name was Kashyap."

"Yes. Originally, I was named Kashyap as a monk. But later, my teacher believed I surpassed the others, and thus I was christened Mahakashyap."

12

The Mystery Deepens

Raj completed his account, and both were looking at him in shock.

"Nobody visited here except Ananya, the minister, and that group of spies. How did that monk come to know about Charan and his full name?" She stared at Anand with a harsh gaze. "I saw you messaging someone when Charan was interrogating us. I hope you and that monk aren't playing any games with us."

Anand was busy talking to his mother on his mobile.

"My story is also killing me," Anand said after finishing the call, "even though it was just a work of fiction, the coincidence of events nailed me. And how did I come to know the full name of that detective? I've been with you since this morning and since that group met us. I'm the one who received a slap in years."

Deepa remained silent for a while, unsure about AK's role in today's chain of events.

"Still, you messaged someone at that time," Deepa said.

"Please, madam. I just messaged one of my friends, who is a reporter, for help, but my message is still unread. I've already checked it." He extended his mobile, but she made no effort to look at it.

"You've just spoken with your mom. I hope everything is well there."

"Yeah. Some other team visited there. They told my mother that they were searching for a thief who had just escaped from jail and entered my apartment," Anand answered briefly.

"Hmm. Your mother is smart. She didn't even need to inform you."

"But my father was also there. Today is Sunday, if you remember," he said, knowing she was still doubting him.

How could she forget? It really had been a long Sunday.

"Listen, madam. Now, it's a fact that we are in trouble. For them, there are only three people who met the monk... please, Ma'am, let me explain. We all know for sure that Raju is the only official person who met the monk. But they doubt that my story is not a work of fiction, thanks to the timing of its revelation."

"And we should be again thankful to your postscript of your story that I am supposed to be the host of the monk this weekend!" Deepa told sarcastically.

"But the most important character of this story now is Rajkamal, the dashing brother of Deepa Kamal. Anand Bhaiya is now losing centre stage, and I am replacing him," Raj said, all smiling.

"And soon you will be hijacked by that team of detectives for further interrogation, and instead of preparing and appearing for your board exams, you will be enjoying your time with them."

In reality, Raj was worried inside. He never expected that an adventurous journey with a monk would soon turn into a nightmare.

"You are right, madam." This time, Anand was serious. "By reason or without, we are now fully involved in this monk business, and I am sure that wherever we go, we will be followed by those detectives. So, it's better to close ourselves behind the wall for some days."

"Just like house arrest!"

"But I am thinking differently. I believe the monk is intentionally involving us in this drama. He intentionally met my brother and tried to introduce himself as the legendary Mahakashyap."

"But Didi, he never tried so. He even told me that he belongs to a village called Gurpa."

"And he said that Gurpa is famous for himself. Gurpa is the place where the great Mahakashyap was buried. Hundreds, if not thousands, of people used to visit that village just to pay homage to him. Some days ago, Mr Anand told me that he wanted to visit this legendary village called Gurpa, where our monk is cremated. And it is a legend that Mahakashyap is waiting under his Samadhi to reincarnate when the future Buddha comes."

Raj was stunned and looked at her with surprise. He had never heard this story before.

"You are right, Ma'am. I wonder how I missed this," Anand expressed his amazement.

"And I also wonder how an ardent follower like AK missed or pretended to miss this point," she said, her voice tinged with suspicion. Anand knew she still doubted him, and understandably so.

"But what is the story of the reincarnation of Mahakashyap?" Raj was still reeling from the revelation. Had he really met a time-travelled monk? His adventurous mind was racing.

"I will tell you this story later. Right now, I'm curious about how the cops let our boy go without questioning him, considering he's the only one who spent time with him."

"Maybe they're listening to us through some hidden device. I've read about such things in detective novels..." Raj joked.

Although Raj said this in jest, Anand and Deepa exchanged looks of utter shock. Was this why the detectives hadn't returned? Were they listening to their conversation?

Deepa's face flushed with anger. Were they still under suspicion, treated like criminals?

Raj realised he might have stumbled upon something significant, even though he'd meant it as a joke.

Suddenly, Deepa burst out laughing.

"Better stop reading thrillers, my brother. Such things only happen in Bond movies. We've been dragged into this drama for nothing. AK, you better go home, get some rest, and let us do the same," she said, starting to rise from her chair.

Both Anand and Raj could tell Deepa was putting on an act.

"Yeah, I'm tired too. I'll head to my flat and take a bath."

"But before you leave, let me check your mobile."

Anand handed over his mobile without any hesitation.

"So, this is their story," Charan told his teammate Verma, switching off his speaker. "Now, what do you have to say?"

"I think the lady and her friends guessed that we were listening to them, so they cut their conversation short. Still, I would give the clear chit to the boy. His statements are already corroborated by nearby shops and CCTV footage. He was indeed with MMK. Even Deepa has nothing to hide but that Anand is still under my suspicion."

"But you have visited his home and already interrogated his parents."

"Still, we cannot be certain about him. After all, he is the one who claimed to have met him. He even invited him to his mentor's house. Then, his mentor's brother was given a lift by MMK."

"And he says that everything is fiction. If he intended to hide his meeting with our man, why would he forward his story?"

"He forwarded his story to Deepa. But it was she who shared it with her circle."

"Hmm. So, you're suggesting that Anand is trying to shelter our man?"

"I'm not saying anything definitively. But I don't want to take any risks. The pressure from above is already mounting to catch him. We should keep our men on all three. I think MMK might try to contact them again."

"But why? Are they a team, or does MMK have something to gain from them?"

They had no answer.

13

The Three Meet Again

"We are being followed the whole way," Anand said.

"And we are followed by high-class spies!" Raj added excitedly.

Anand and Deepa smiled at each other. Yesterday, Anand departed without further discussions when they became sure that they had been heard. Raj easily found an electronic device below the centre table, and Deepa didn't hesitate to throw it outside.

"Are you sure that we are not heard from here?" Deepa asked.

"Yeah. That is for sure. You finalised this location after coming out of your home. So, no chance of a pre-planted camera or any device," Anand said with a smile.

"Yeah. Actually, I have decided to meet here because Sharma lives here alone. He would return only by evening."

"Is he the same one who picked up your brother from the Bodhgaya office?"

"Yes, Bhai. Still, everything is possible. After all, we are dealing with an enlightened monk."

"Not enlightened. We are dealing with a fraud," there was bitterness in her voice. "A damn damn fraud, who not only involved me but also my brother."

"So, you think he gave me a lift for some reason?"

"I am sure about that. Last night, Ananya sent me a clip of CCTV where MMK dropped my brother. He looks intentionally at the CCTV so that he could easily be recognised."

"And what purpose would be solved for him with that? Is he challenging that team of detectives or challenging the government?"

"I am not sure. But he surely has a purpose, and every step of his is intentional."

"But what purpose does he want to solve by involving Raj or you?"

"Because he is pretending to be historical Mahakashyap, and I am the only one in the entire university who has done a PhD on Mahakashyap."

He looked at her surprisingly. It was a revelation for him that she had done her thesis on Mahakashyap.

"So, you think he wants recognition from you?"

"What else could be the reason, AK?"

"If that's the reason, why hasn't MMK approached you directly till now? Why is he playing a hide-and-seek game with the police? If he is moving freely, why is it reported that he is missing? Why is that Tibetan man so serious about his whereabouts? Why did he spend his time with your brother sharing his knowledge? And who was that mystery man who informed him about those detectives?"

"Lots of questions, Bhai. But I could answer only one correctly," Raj said mischievously.

Both stared at him.

"I know about that mystery man. He is Rajesh Sharma, a local ASI."

"But yesterday you told us that MMK didn't..."

"Easy, Bhai. It's true that he didn't allow me to touch his mobile, but unfortunately, instead of searching for his contact, he typed his number. And I guessed the number from the movement of his hand."

Both looked at him with astonishment. The boy was turning into Sherlock Holmes!

Raj continued,

"Although Mahakashyap was using an iPhone, his typing speed was very slow, so I easily guessed the number. And luckily, it was in my mind."

"Oh, then we could try to find the owner of the number."

"This is the first thing I did when I was able to repair my phone. And he is Rajesh Sharma ISI, as I mentioned earlier."

Deepa looked at her brother with full praise.

"So, the monk came to know about Charan and his team!"

"Now, we should inform Ananya Didi about his link with Mahakashyap. I even suspect that ASI is helping the monk hide somewhere."

"You may be right, dear, but I don't think it's the right time to reveal anything to the SP," Anand seemed to be pondering something else. "We're not dealing with some local crime. We don't even know who's playing on which side. We don't even know if this Mahakashyap is a villain or something else. It's also possible that this ASI is acting under her instructions."

"But she is Didi's friend..." Raj tried to interrupt.

"No, Bhai. I think AK is correct. Yes, she is my friend, but she is a cop first. I've known Rajesh Sharma for years, and I can easily say that he is Ananya's man. It's possible he's acting on her direction."

Raju was still pondering the monk he met yesterday. He found him utterly wise and couldn't think of him as a rogue. He was also unable to see Ananya Singh as anything other than what she seemed to be.

"So, you both are considering the Mahakashyap I met yesterday as a conspirator and Ananya Didi or that ASI as someone who might be helping him."

"Listen, dear, I'm not saying that exactly. I'm just saying that nobody is beyond suspicion. We've even been put under surveillance by that team of government spies, and that's why they're following us, waiting for the moment when that monk will try to contact us."

"And that monk might try to meet us, bypassing Charan and co.," Deepa suggested. "And if that's true, let's go to the house of the ASI and request a meeting with the monk."

Anand looked at her, bewildered.

"We are followed by Charan's team. Mahakashyap will never come to meet us while we are followed. First, we need to ditch them, and only then should we approach him. But before taking any step, I want to say something," Anand suddenly said, his tone serious.

"I know what you want to say. I also realise that we are working on a hypothesis. There are possibilities that MMK met my brother by chance and that MMK has some old acquaintance with ASI without any intention to contact us. He might have heard my name through some contacts and shown interest in meeting me just as a courtesy call, just as you wrote the article without any ill intention," she smiled.

"You never miss an opportunity to roast me," he replied in a lighter vein; this time, he didn't mind what she said.

"No, AK. I'm not roasting you. Now, I'm trying to believe you because you're equally worried with us. But I want to come out of this matter as soon as possible. I have a good reputation not only in my university but also in this town. Not only my well-wishers but also my neighbours contacted me all night, asking if the raid in my quarters was done by the IT department. Even the Vice-Chancellor telephoned me twice about my well-being. And then those news correspondents; I am dodging them all. So first, I want to meet that monk at any cost."

Raj, who had been listening to the conversation without intervening, suddenly exclaimed excitedly,

"Let's gate-crash his quarters. Or try some back-gate entry!"

"For what? As thieves? My dear, we are not professionals. We can't do such things."

"So, what should we do? Request an appointment?"

"Why not? What's wrong with it? After all, you are a respected lady of the town and have been disturbed by the unlawful activity by Charan and co!"

"Are you joking? Their SP was also with them. And if I'm in any trouble, I'm expected to go to the local police station, not to the house of an ASI. Even if we approach his quarters for no reason, Charan will also follow us there. There's a fair chance that our monk is hiding there, and I don't want to lead Charan and his team to him."

"So, better we request the ASI for an appointment over the phone."

But there was no need. Deepa's mobile started ringing.

"Hello madam, I am Rajesh Sharma, local ASI. I've just received your mobile number... I want to meet you... Actually, a monk is waiting for you at my residence... It's urgent... yes, it relates to yesterday's event... please do not inform anyone, not even Ananya madam... yes, I know she is your friend... please come alone... a car will be at your home within 15 minutes... okay, in 30 minutes, please note the number of the car... yes, the driver will bring you to my quarters."

Deepa looked at both with a smile, "I think our guesses were right. The time has come. Our man is waiting for me. Let me proceed."

"But, Didi, I don't think you should go alone. We don't know who will be there with him. At least let Anand Bhai go with you." There was concern in his voice.

"No, Bhai. I will go alone. If there is any problem, I will send an SOS. You will receive the SOS message simultaneously. You will stay with AK during this time."

As a precaution, Deepa, along with Raj and Anand, had activated the single-button SOS mode on their mobiles.

"And what about Charan's team?"

"No need to worry. Let them do their work. You do yours, and I will do mine."

"I'm meeting the ASI. Where are you going?"

"Taking some precautionary measures. Please delay your meeting for at least one hour."

"And Raju?"

"He will be with me. I'll send him home safely soon."

14

Trapped in a House

It was a typical D type government quarter, an old build, a small campus with the usual lane of flower and vegetable plants on both sides, leading to a veranda. A servant led her to the drawing room and went inside. Deepa relaxed on a sofa, playing with her mobile.

The person who entered the room after a while was certainly not the ASI. Raj had shown her some of his pictures on his Facebook profile. This man was different. She was even sure that this man was not Indian. Chinese? Three more goon-type persons followed him into the room.

Was she stuck among bad people? She looked at the door. Could she have the necessity to flee the room? Or was it time to push SOS on her mobile? She felt genuinely frightened.

"Sorry, madam, if I scared you. I used Rajesh's mobile to call you here."

She recognised his voice easily. He was the person to whom she had talked. He continued,

"Believe me, we are not bad people. I am also a follower of Buddha. I have great respect for an educated scholar like you and would never think of harming you."

He spoke very clear Hindi without a hint of a foreign accent.

"Where is Rajesh? Who are you?"

"Oh, I should have mentioned first. My name is Chaini. But I am Indian, you know. Unfortunately, my mother was from China, so some think of me as Chinese due to my small nose and eyes. You know, even Chinese always love India and especially your Bodhgaya, the holy town where Buddha attained Nirvana, so they visit here regularly. Rajesh is inside. He is my friend. But unfortunately, he is not feeling well, so he's taking some rest. But I could see you seemed to be tense."

"Why don't you ask your friend to come outside if he is here?"

"Oh, he would not be interested in sitting with me. Actually, we had a fight. You know, good friends always fight," he stopped with a small laugh.

She looked at him. On another day, she might have found this man with an average height and slim structure very friendly, but for some reason, the environment in the room made her uneasy. Or was it his three staff members that she was afraid of? She knew that getting out of here as soon as possible was the better option. She spoke, making her voice firmer,

"Okay, sir, please tell me how I can help you."

"Oh, don't call me sir," he said, as if embarrassed, "I'm not such a big deal. Just call me Chaini."

Now, she felt irritated by his tone but kept herself calm.

"Okay, let me explain. Actually, I've been searching for one of my uncles for some days. You know, although he is a very simple man, sometimes he pretends to be a disciple of Bhagwan Buddha."

She now knew whose name he was about to mention. He continued,

"But 'pretend' is the wrong word. Actually, he believes he is Mahakashyap, a 2500-year-old monk who lived at the time of Buddha. You know Mahakashyap? Oh, sorry, I just forgot that I am speaking to a scholar like you. I'm sure you know him better than me."

"Yes, I've heard his name," she said slowly.

"Yes. But you know, my friend told me a while ago that he hadn't heard his name. And can you imagine, my uncle, whose actual name is Kashyap, was hiding here for some days? And Rajesh didn't inform me! So, we had a fight, and I gave him a good punch. But you know, it's usual between friends." He chuckled.

She could sense the cruelty hidden in his voice. Was he trying to intimidate her?

"But how can I help you here?"

"Oh, I see how simple you are. You should have guessed that the person who yesterday gave your brother a lift was my uncle himself. Isn't it amazing that I'm searching for my uncle everywhere, and he was enjoying a ride with your brother? And sometimes enjoying time with Rajesh. So funny!"

She thought of pressing the SOS button but stopped herself. Lest her brother and AK come here and get trapped!

"But yesterday, we came to know that not only the local police but also central agencies are trying to catch him."

"The same story again! But before that, please allow me to hold your mobile. It's distracting our conversation, you know." He almost snatched her mobile and continued speaking, shaking his head, "Even Rajesh was repeating the same story. Everyone's confusing my uncle with someone else. My uncle is a simple villager. Yes, he has some good knowledge of Buddhism, and that's all. So please tell me where he is."

"But how could I know where he is? He left my brother yesterday at Shaheed Chowk and then went missing."

"But your brother didn't tell you anything else? My uncle was always interested in meeting you. Rajesh told me he was very keen to meet you. He should have contacted you."

"No, sir. You can check my mobile. Or better check Rajesh's mobile. There should be a contact number for him." Suddenly, it occurred to her that Rajesh's mobile would likely have MMK's contact number. After all, he contacted Rajesh right in front of Raj.

"Oh, you don't know my friend. He formatted his mobile just before I arrived here and now can't even recall his number. You know how much slavish these friends are."

She now understood that neither Rajesh was his friend nor the monk his uncle. Clearly, he was desperate to find the monk at any cost. She even doubted whether Rajesh was still alive. Now, she only wanted to get away from this madman.

"Okay, sir. Please give me your mobile number. I'll inform you whenever your uncle contacts me."

"Oh, that's okay. But I can't remember my number either. Still, you can call me on my friend's number. You know Rajesh is my friend." He still didn't give up appearing gentlemanly. His staff stood behind him, expressionless. "But what if you forget to inform me? You know, I love my uncle so much. Why not leave your brother with me? I swear he'll have a good time here."

"Hello," she almost roared, "I have been tolerating your nonsense for some time. Be smart, but don't be too smart. Don't mess with my brother."

"Oh, but I've already asked my friends to bring your brother here. But I should have asked you first. My mistake. I think your brother will be arriving soon. Oh, just forgot, I even asked them to bring that student of yours; otherwise, your brother will feel lonely. Gaur, please call Billu. Don't know why they are so late."

She saw this as her chance to escape before her brother and Anand arrived, as Chaini was distracted talking to his men. She had already confirmed that the outer gate was still unlocked. Perhaps they hadn't expected her to try escaping.

She couldn't recall ever moving with such agility. Before they could react, she was out of the room, slamming the door shut behind her with shaking hands.

She was running out of the room without calculating what was happening behind her. Then, there was a strong hit on her head, and she started falling.

She could remember the face of Anand entering from the main gate with an unknown face before falling unconscious.

She could feel her whole body aching as she started regaining consciousness. She was handcuffed from behind, her head resting on someone's shoulder.

It was Anand, who was also handcuffed. Shen was still seated in front of her.

"Where is Raj? I left him with you," she whispered, trying to sit up properly.

"I don't know. We were returning to your home, but he found someone and took the lift, leaving me alone. I was on my way home when these men caught me," Anand said. She could tell from his voice that he had been manhandled badly.

"So careless, your boyfriend. Couldn't even look after your brother properly."

"Mind your language. I am not her boyfriend. She is a respectable professor," Anand retorted, then looking at Deepa, asked, "And who is this joker? Cooking me for a while."

She felt a little stronger seeing him. She had entrusted her brother to him, and she could guess that he wouldn't have left him unsecured. She then said,

"I don't know him well. His uncle is missing, and he is suspecting us."

"And my uncle's name is Kashyap," he continued, still pretending to be someone concerned about his missing uncle. "And now Raj is also missing, you don't know. I am also worried about him."

"Stop playing the fool, man. Damn liar you are," Anand interrupted. "Raj must be safe. Let us go safely; otherwise, you will be in trouble. We have nothing to do with your uncle."

"You guys are such liars, not me," Chaini retorted, becoming emotional again. "You wrote a piece about your interaction with my uncle, and now you're calling me a liar. That boy spent a whole day with my uncle. And then last night, my uncle paid a visit to your girlfriend – oh, sorry, my mistake – to your teacher, and you're still pleading innocence. Tell me, which nephew wouldn't feel upset?"

He looked at her with surprise.

"This man is confused or has the wrong information. Even now, I am interested in meeting him, but he never contacted me."

"That is really amazing, ma'am. After yesterday's drama at your home, I installed a camera facing your entrance. But believe me, it was just to track the movement of outsiders like my uncle. You know my uncle! But unfortunately, I only checked the recordings this morning! And you know, your brother let him in! He was inside for not less than two hours! And still, you are trying to fool me! Liars!" He was again getting emotional. "Bablu, release the handcuffs of both and let them see the recordings."

Both were looking at the recordings with extreme surprise.

It was another shocker of the week. So, was Raj playing a hide-and-seek game with them? Did he get Rajesh Sharma's number directly from the monk and not by chance?

Perhaps he has been in direct contact with the monk since yesterday? Or even before? What magic had that man cast on him?

"Isn't it like that your brother is playing some games even with you both?" he said, seeing the surprised faces of both.

This was when someone from outside came running into the room informing him that a police jeep carrying a police team had already entered the lane. Before Chaini could understand anything, the policemen entered the quarter with double speed.

15

Anand Takes the Lead

"You should now feel relaxed. The main culprit and his goons are behind bars, and your sister, along with Anand, is completely safe," Kashyap told Raj, entering his room.

Raj ran and hugged him tightly.

"But I accept that it was just due to me that they ran into trouble. I told you yesterday to arrange a meeting with your sister at Rajesh's house. Meanwhile, I got information this morning that that Chinese scoundrel was coming there to catch me, so I escaped from there. Unfortunately, Rajesh messed with them and was seriously injured."

"Yeah, I tried to reach you on mobile, but yours was switched off. Then you called me from another number, and I informed you that my sister was going to meet you, but unfortunately, she fell into the hands of that scoundrel."

"All is well that ends well. Ananya acted very swiftly on your call—a rarity for some in the Indian Police."

Raj breathed a sigh of relief. Had he not received MMK's call, his sister would have been in great trouble. MMK informed him that Chaini was a real scoundrel working on the payroll of some Chinese secret services. He had also told Kashyap that the police and detectives were using the word MMK for him, and he immediately liked it.

"But I still don't understand why these people were against you. I understand that Chaini was working on the orders of some Chinese agency to abduct you. But why? What have you done to them?"

MMK smiled.

"It wasn't just an attempt to abduct, dear. They wanted to kill me because they think I'm dangerous."

Raj looked at him in surprise. How could this grand old man be dangerous to anyone!

"You are confusing me, Uncle. Please stop speaking in riddles. My sister said that you are pretending to be the historical Mahakashyap and that you want recognition from her." He felt no need to hide anything from him.

The monk chuckled softly.

"That's why I've been saying from the start that your sister is wonderful."

She was still in shock; it had truly been a narrow escape. She looked at Ananya with gratitude. Ananya smiled,

"You should be more thankful to your brother. It was he who informed me that you and Anand were being held captive by that scoundrel. You should know that he was not a simple criminal. He was a regular offender, and we had been after him for years. He never thought he would be caught so easily. He even overpowered our ASI with ease."

"How is he now?" Anand asked. They were sitting in the chamber of SP Ananya Singh.

"Recovering. But I still can't understand how your brother knew about Chaini, especially since he said that he snatched your mobile."

Both looked at each other, realising it was now necessary to inform her about everything.

"It was the monk who informed him about everything."

"You mean Mahakashyap?" She almost jumped from her chair.

She nodded and explained everything.

"Actually, Raj was with me when madam left us in the morning. But he also left, saying he was going to meet a friend. But now I think he had some plan and went to meet the monk."

"So, MMK was staying with our ASI and left when he knew Chaini was approaching. This man never lets anyone live in peace."

"But why was that scoundrel after the monk? He even claimed the monk was his uncle!"

"He's the most irritating man. He even told me he's a responsible citizen and that Deepa Kamal was trying to abduct him."

Anand burst out laughing but quickly controlled himself, earning a glare from Deepa.

"Sorry, but why was he after the monk?"

"Actually, he's a contract killer and works for money. We're still not sure who's behind him, but we'll find out soon. First, tell me, have you tried contacting your brother?"

"Yes, as soon as I got my mobile back from Chaini, I started calling him but received no response except for a text saying, 'My battery is draining out, and I'll contact you soon.'"

"I have also tried to contact him, but his mobile is still switched off," Anand said.

"I can see that you're becoming restless without your mobile. Don't become so dependent on anything."

He giggled.

"I was just worried about my sister. She might be getting anxious."

"Soon you'll be with your sister. Be patient. Currently, she's discussing matters with the SP. Anand is also there."

"But I won't leave this house until you clear my doubts." He insisted like a child. They were relaxing in an old building in old Gaya, also known as Ander Gaya. Though Raj had been in Gaya for some years, he'd never had a chance to visit this part of the city. "I also wonder how you find such places to hide."

"After Banaras, Gaya is the most undiscovered city. And regarding your doubt, I will try to answer one or two."

"Then tell me first, you seem to be alone, yet you get any information you want with such ease. Last time, it was Rajesh Sharma ASI. But how did you come to know that my Didi is in trouble? Now, you have been with me for a while, and you are still informing me that Didi and Anand Bhaiya are sitting with the SP. Is it a sixth sense or some other vidya?"

He laughed for some time, then whispered mysteriously,

"Leave something undisclosed for this old man." Then, in his usual voice, "But you should know, nothing is supernatural in this world. Everything is defined by natural laws. When we are unable to define the law, we call it supernatural. In the past, we couldn't explain the rain and attributed it to supernatural powers. But now, even a sixth-grade student can explain how the rain happens. The same is true for our mind and body. Most of us still can't use the power of the mind properly. The same is true about the capability of our body. Breathe properly, and a hundred or five hundred will become just a number, not an age."

"But what will one do if someone puts a bullet in our body!" Raj said mischievously.

"I understand what you're trying to say," the monk replied, "What will happen if someone like Chaini puts a bullet into my body? Yes, the body will die. But do you think that life is limited to this body only? No, dear! Even Buddha says that he attained Nirvana after millions of births."

"I heard that his chief disciple Mahakashyap lived for more than one hundred and twenty years!"

"I think you got that information from your sister. But you're right."

"No, uncle. I got that information from Google. Yesterday, I was checking the internet about Mahakashyap and got a lot of unusual information. It was even written that he was buried at the village Gurpa. And you mentioned earlier that you're from the same village. And your name is also Mahakashyap. Don't you want to say that you are the ancient Mahakashyap?"

"Yes, he is, but in a new body," said the man who just entered the room.

Raj was really surprised to see him here. He had met him before.

"Give me his number," Ananya requested.

Deepa wrote it on a piece of paper. Ananya exited the room with the paper.

"She'll try to track him," Anand said.

"But his mobile is switched off."

"His last location can be tracked. They have their methods. I think she'll also inform Charan and his team."

"Let them do their work. I'm only worried about Raju. He is my world. I'll be held responsible if anything happens to him. Hopefully, Charan has a different way to track him."

Her voice became hoarse. It was the first time Anand saw her so emotional. She again tried to contact her brother. He was still out of range.

Within five minutes, Ananya re-entered the room with Charan. This time, he was alone. Charan took a chair and positioned himself between Anand and Deepa. Ananya resumed her usual seat behind the desk.

"Sorry, gentleman," he said, shaking hands with Anand, "and sorry for everything, madam. That small story created so much havoc. Even our seniors were convinced after reading it that you were responsible for his hideout. Sometimes, we get so influenced by our seniors that we stop thinking for ourselves. And all this for a simple monk."

"Any information about my brother, sir?" Deepa asked.

"Don't worry. We'll find him soon. I don't know how that stupid monk has managed to influence your brother."

"Yeah. His mobile is still switched off."

"Not just switched off. I think the scoundrel instructed the boy to remove the SIM card."

"You're too critical of the monk," Ananya commented with a smile.

"To hell with his Monk-giri. I don't know why we give him so much attention. Excuse me."

Charan was now on a call. As he spoke, his face grew pale. After ending the call, his voice was no longer loud or assertive. Rising from his chair, he said, "Okay, friends. My job here is done. I need to go."

"But what actually happened?" Ananya inquired.

"This MMK must be a Chinese agent. Our department has known about him for a while, but we have no proof. And about his claims, although I'm not a student of history or Buddhism, it's written somewhere that the future Buddha Maitreya will soon come, and an old disciple of Buddha named Mahakashyap will be reborn to announce his arrival. That way, the scoundrel could gain the public's sympathy, not just from Buddhists but also from Hindus, as the concept of Maitreya is also popular in Hinduism."

"But who would believe such a nonsensical story? And that Tibetan minister mentioned that Chinese agencies were trying to abduct or kill him."

"That fucking minister was the real scoundrel. He was with the MMK from the start. All his stories were nonsense. He was either the mastermind or MMK was fooling him. Our people are so sentimental; they're always ready to believe such nonsense. I even hired a goon to block him, but our SP madam disrupted our plan. We have news that they've created a small group of people all over India to spread this rumour." So, it was Charan for whom Chaini was working!

"So, we have to stop this agent anyhow," Deepa said.

"We are already late, madam. Some national news channels have already picked up this news and started broadcasting it. Kashyap and that Tibetan minister will be on the news channels soon. And to support his claim, they are also showing documentary evidence in the form of a thesis written by some idiot years ago," Charan said, keeping an eye on Deepa.

She was literally stunned. She murmured after some time, "But I only quoted some scriptures..."

Now she understood why they were after her. She had written about the reincarnation of Mahakashyap and that Maitreya in detail.

"Still, I can't understand how our whole intelligence is admitting defeat to these two monks," Ananya Singh said. "Just give me two hours, and these two crooks will disappear forever."

Charan laughed softly as if mocking himself, "Do you think there are only two? Just visit Bodhgaya, and you'll find each and every follower chanting the name of Mahakashyap. The seed of MMK was sown long ago. Even now, they are distributing photos and posters of MMK for the event on the 23rd, when Buddhists from most parts of the world will join them."

"But what's on the 23rd… Oh my God!" How could she forget! She was a prime guest for the Buddha Purnima celebrations!

Deepa was also shocked. She had been invited to the event too. She looked at AK, who was smiling. What was going on in his mind?

"They have chosen the best day. Even if Kashyap can't join them, the cult of MMK will work for them."

"Perfectly said, sir. At least China will be able to put a figure parallel to the Dalai Lama! All these years, China was unable to downplay the Dalai Lama. Now, the cult of MMK will work for them," Anand said with a suspenseful smile.

"Now I can say you are the most intelligent among us. That's why our government is downplaying the matter. In India, you can do anything but not play with sentiments.

That's why we hired a goon to kill Kashyap before the news of MMK spread all over," Charan said with a faint smile on his lips.

Deepa now understood the gravity of the situation.

After a while, Deepa spoke again, "But where is Raju? Still no news from him."

This time, Anand spoke but in a different, firmer tone, "Don't worry, madam. Your Raju is safe. And Mr. Charan, you needn't worry either. Kashyap will surrender his claims soon. Let's go. We have to meet our men. On the way, we will have some discussions."

Even Deepa couldn't understand AK's changing tone. There was definitely something he knew better than her and all.

"I really appreciate your interest in the religion of Tathagat, even at this tender age. But never fall into the trap of your Google uncle. There is a lot of information, but first, authenticate it with scripture. They are the real Buddha. If you want a real Buddha in your study, better use scriptures, like Tripitaka, instead of his idols," said the person who just entered the room.

"Yeah, sometimes statues of Buddha also remind us of our eternal goal, but if you want to know him, become offline and follow his scripture," said the MMK.

He didn't know what to say. He was never a Buddhist, except that he loved to sit near the large statue of Buddha in Bodhgaya. Still, he said, "But scriptures are hard to understand. They are very complicated." There were lots of Buddhist literature in his house, thanks to his sister, but he never managed to read more than 5-6 pages. He found them boring.

"You are right, dear. I understand what you want to say. There are multiple explanations. I know you are too young to understand the Tripitaka. But when one Buddha himself starts delivering, even a kid will understand his words."

"But Buddha is history and…"

"Yes, boy, Buddha is history, but Buddhahood is not. We are very fortunate that another Buddha is coming!"

"Yes! He is coming!" Kashyap repeated his words. Both folded their hands. There was utter reverence on both of their faces.

He could assume that both of them were not pretending. But whose arrival were they talking about? He felt that he was stuck among some fools. All he could say was, "May I go for now?"

"Sure, dear. But my desire to meet your sister is still incomplete. However, I think we will be called for in the newsroom with your sister soon for some detailed discussion," the monk said.

16

The Trap

"So, at last, we have the privilege of meeting you!" he says. "Mr. Kashyap, in his own flesh and blood, enjoying his solitude."

"Don't call it solitude, sir," Kashyap replied with his usual smile. "Mr. Raju has been keeping me good company. Even my old friend Saran is now with me for a few hours. But I should apologise to you all for keeping you busy. I told Saran earlier to keep calm for a few more days, but he unnecessarily involved your team over a simple monk like me."

"Thanks for calling me your friend. You are not a simple monk," his voice shaking with gratitude. "You don't know how important you are for all of us. Our privilege is that we are presently sharing this space with you. Who knows, within months, millions of people will dream of meeting you. We all were worried about you. When we learned that some miscreants were following you, we tried our best to protect you. Now, I should be thankful to Charan sir and SP madam for apprehending the team of culprits."

"All grace to Lord Maitreya. And we should apologise to Deepa madam and Anand Kumar. They were unnecessarily involved in this case. Please accept my sincere apologies." Kashyap folded his hands.

Sitting in a corner seat, Raju was in full dilemma. Could it be possible that Mr. Kashyap or Sharan was a culprit or conspirator, as Anand had told him? He had been with them for some time. He couldn't say anything about Mr. Saran, but he found Mr. Kashyap very knowledgeable and generous. Although he didn't like deceiving a great monk like him, he was still following Anand Bhaiya's direction. He had shared the location with him before switching off his mobile. But how could he forget that the lives of his sister and Anand were saved due to the intervention of the monk?

It was an old-style drawing room with scattered chairs and three large bookshelves. An old, large sofa occupied by Charan, who had a Bluetooth headset in his ears, along with Deepa and Anand, faced the old Kashyap. Ananya Singh and Saran were also present.

"I also want to submit my apology to Mr. Anand for my misbehaviour. I was not informed that he was a senior intelligence officer working directly under the control of the ministry. He even wrote that story so that the culprits would start following him and could be easily caught. Thanks to his leads, we have been able to capture a significant international gang in Bodhgaya!" Happiness was visible on Charan's face.

Everyone was shocked by the news. It was news to Deepa too. Anand had been with her for many days, but she had never expected that he was something else. Raju was also stunned.

"Sorry to all. It was a secret mission. I've been working on it for months. I've had some success, but the main culprit is still on the run," Deepa realised he was a different Anand.

"I am also working on some leads. I hope to succeed soon. But I can see Mr Kashyap also seems tense. Not a good sign for a senior monk like you, sir," Charan added.

"Do not confuse compassion with tension, sir," said Saran, the Tibetan minister, intervening. "A monk of his calibre is never tense."

"Let him speak, dear. I still wonder why there are so many good things to do, yet some people always indulge in dirty things. They cannot understand our emotions or our way of life. There are people who are creating disharmony among us, but we have to create a different world. Let them do their work, and we will do ours."

"That should be the religious way of thinking, sir. But now we should part ways as we have a lot to do. You know Buddha Purnima is near. So, allow us to depart if we are not under arrest," Saran said with a slight laugh.

"Never, sir. Who could arrest a monk like you? Yes, sometimes we have to undertake unreligious works, but I have always had great respect for Buddha and his teachings," Ananya stated.

"Yes, sir. Putting our job aside, I am a great admirer of Buddha. It is our privilege to have spent some time with you. Soon, you will be busy with your work, and I will be with mine. Why not have some discussions with Deepa madam about your work and also satisfy our curiosity? You have expressed a desire to meet Deepa madam, as Raju has told us," Anand said to Kashyap, smiling at Deepa.

"Yes, I am interested, Anand sir," Deepa said, addressing him formally for the first time—after all, he was an officer.

"I would also be pleased to hear him. But better next time. There are important meetings in Bodhgaya," Saran said, preparing to get up.

"Please, sir. No meetings will begin until Mr Kashyap arrives. After all, he is such an important person now," Raju interjected, feeling odd as he watched even Charan make such requests.

"Okay, sir. There are hectic schedules from tomorrow, and I would love to have a discussion with a learned lady like you."

"As you wish. I am surrendering to your wish. But allow me some time. I need to make a call to my team for the evening. I also have to inform our ministry about the well-being of Mahakashyap. I will be here soon."

"Please, sir. But you didn't need permission from anyone. Even if we tried to stop you, our government would twist our ears. After all, you hold an equivalent position in the Tibetan Government-in-exile."

Everyone laughed out loud, the atmosphere in the room becoming positive. The minister took a bow and left the room.

"So, let us discuss. Enlighten me with your knowledge, madam."

Deepa smiled, "Don't call it a discussion, sir. My knowledge is limited to some books, and you are a learned Buddhist."

"I do not agree with the term Buddhist, Ma'am. Anyone who converts to our religion is known as a Buddhist. And there are more than fifty crore people in the world who are known as followers of Buddhism. But their devotion is limited to some rituals without following the essence of Buddha's teachings."

There was an expression of admiration in her eyes. Clearly, he was not a conservative follower.

"And what is the path of Buddha?"

"Are you kidding me, madam?" Kashyap was all smiles. "His teaching is available and known even to a layman or school student. Do you still think that it needs another explanation from me? Your history books are full of works on it. And if we set aside the literary works, there are monasteries where Buddhist Tripitaka has been taught. There are also meditation centres all over, and if you ask me, every meditation method is attributed to the Tathagat. If you do not want to go anywhere, your mobile provides everything you want through Wikipedia and YouTube. Correct me if I am wrong."

Anand now could see a winning smile on the face of Deepa, his mentor. Oh, she looked really cute!

"Yes, sir. How true you are. Everything is available online and offline for seekers. There is the School of the Elders as Theravada, then there is Mahayana, and for Tantrika practitioners, there is Vajrayana. Everything is available. And if we want something else in Buddhism, there are four Tibetan schools. Still, do you think we require another set of principles of Buddhism? Another living Buddha in the form of Maitreya?"

"Easy, madam, easy," Anand thought. "Don't hit so hard. We need some more time."

Everyone could see that there was complete blankness on Kashyap's face for a while. After some time, he began speaking again,

"I like your frankness, madam. You are right. But that is the beauty of Buddhism. It was never a stagnant religion. Wherever it went, it adapted to the local environments. In some parts of India, it adopted the tantric environment and became Vajrayana. It went to Tibet and mixed itself with the local Bon religion and became Lama Buddhism. It went to Japan and China, mixed with their local religions, and evolved into something new. Still, the core teaching of the Tathagat is available everywhere."

"I wonder if Lord Buddha would have agreed with these new forms of their teachings. Idol worship of him or Tantric Buddha," Anand speaks in a low voice.

"We must always be ready for anything new," says Kashyap. "But you must know that even after all these years and centuries, there is one thing still in common in each and every form of Buddhism."

"And what is that?" asks Deepa.

"Lord Maitreya. As the successor of Lord Buddha." It seemed as if a divine aura had appeared not only on his face but also in the room. Raju also remembered that there was the same aura on his face while he was talking earlier in the presence of Saran, the minister.

"And you think that the time has already come for the advent of Lord Maitreya?"

"Yes. The time has come." Everyone could see that his confidence was at a different level.

"And how can you say so? Different scriptures show different timescales." It was Anand who asked.

"Set aside all the scriptures. The time has come. And who will know better than me? Better than Kashyap. Better than the eternal Mahakashyap!" It seems that someone else was talking from his body.

Suddenly, Deepa's eyes went towards Charan, still with his Bluetooth headset, who was giving Anand some signal through hand gestures.

"Please allow me to stop this interesting discussion for a while and put a question to Mr Kashyap." And without a break, he continues, "You should know that there were rumours of the involvement of Chinese machinery in this Mahakashyap, or we may say MMK business. We also get the news that you or Mr Saran are Chinese agents or being used by them." Anand told firmly.

"Thanks for being so clear. Now I know that you are working for the government, and you have every right to protect your country."

"Sorry to interrupt, but the country is also yours. You should be cooperative during all interrogations."

"Always, sir. I have huge respect for my country," the monk said, bowing his head. "If you find a single piece of evidence of me disrespecting the country or even if you find that I am being used by any foreign country, I will lose the right to live."

"Thanks for the cooperation, sir. We are not sure about you yet, but we just got some concrete evidence against Mr Saran, the Tibetan minister. Thanks to Mr Anand and his bluffs regarding some international gang in Bodhgaya, Mr Saran became attentive. He went to his car and started contacting his contacts in China and in Bodhgaya. We have already placed some online devices in his car, and we have some good recordings. I was listening to everything through my earphones, and everything is already recorded. Although it is in Chinese, and I have very limited knowledge of it. But I think you are very good at it."

Switching the speaker on, Charan put his mobile on the nearby table. Although SP Ananya Singh, Anand Kumar, Deepa Kamal, or even Rajkamal alias Raju were completely alien to this language, they could understand every bit of the word coming out of the mobile by the expression on the face of the monk called Kashyap.

17

All Is Well That Ends Well

"So now I could say that all is well that ends well!"

"Don't say so, Raju. I am not feeling well for Kashyap. I still think he was a nice soul, and rejected his claim when he came to know about Saran. Still, he was arrested. Even he didn't oppose his arrest."

"I still have some doubt. If he was not the same MMK, why did he claim to be so?"

"Because he was made to believe so," Deepa said. "Listen, it was just like the Godman concept. Self-deception is the most dangerous concept. You will find lots of Kalki Avatars in India because their disciples made them believe. And then they started believing so. Just like if I started to say that you are the most handsome boy in the town, you would believe it."

"But I am," Raju said with his usual mischievous smile.

"The same became true for Kashyap. Yes, he was really a learned monk, and Gurpa was his hometown. But when he met Saran, he must have found a good partner for his project.

He would have made him believe that he was the eternal Mahakashyap, now in a new body. The concept of rebirth is always prevailing in Buddhism."

"But the masterstroke was by Anand Bhaiya. I also started believing that he was a real intelligence officer. Even I started dreaming of him as Bond with guns in both hands."

"Don't say so. Otherwise, he will start believing it, and I will lose a good student."

Anand was all smiles. Deepa was praising him. He could see that she felt a little shy while praising him. Or was it his imagination?

"I heard Mr Charan saying that ours would be a great team. Why don't we form a detective team! RAD detectives!" Raju said.

"First, do some makeup work for your exam. You have already lost some important days," Deepa told him.

"Yes, Didi. But one last question from Bhai. How did you come to know that Saran was playing some game? Did you really write that story intentionally? Because that story played an important role in finding the culprit."

Instead of Anand, Deepa said,

"I know Ak will not accept anything. He will continue to say that he wrote that story without knowing anything. But whatever he says, I know he was hiding something. He was a step ahead of us from the beginning."

18

A Buddha in the Study Part III

"I can see you are still feeling sorry for Kashyap."

"Yes, sir. I think he was a nice soul."

"Yes, he was, and he is. But when you are on the path of purification, you should not let others control you. He may not be out of jail soon, but he will soon realise where he went wrong."

"Then how can we judge ourselves to ensure we are on the right path?"

"To judge is not good, Anand Kumar. When you start judging someone or even yourself, you have preconceived notions of good and bad. Never be prejudiced. Have you ever observed your mind? Your mind with lust or your mind with greed? Or your mind without lust sometimes or your mind without greed sometimes? No, sir. You always start judging. You never observe your mind; instead, you start calculating."

"But what is the role of the mind if it cannot judge?"

"First, you should know that we start judging based on preconceived assumptions of good or bad. But a religious mind should be fresh and always ready to accept anything new."

He was sitting on the same cot, beside my study table, speaking as usual.

"Kashyap has an unusual brain. He mastered every Buddhist scripture and meditated regularly. But he had some preconceived notions about Buddhism and Maitreya. Therefore, he easily fell into the trap of another intelligent person."

"Earlier, you were praising the greatness and importance of scriptures. Now you are saying that scriptures are preconceived notions."

"I'm not saying that, dear. Scriptures are a way to understand something higher. But never fall into their trap."

"So, the concept of Maitreya is a trap?"

"What are you saying, dear! Maitreya is not merely a concept. As long as humanity has the possibility to attain Nirvana, Maitreya is there. Maitreya is the highest possibility of humanity!"

"Just like Buddha!"

"Yes, just like Buddha."

"So Maitreya is not a person, but a state!"

"No, sir. Just as Buddha is a historical person and also a state, so too is Maitreya a future person and a state."

"Hmm. I understand what you're saying, but only as a theory. But still, I didn't understand something. Why did you approach me to solve this matter? Even you told me that I am the first person who met Tathagat in his lifetime."

"Because of your love for me. You love Mahakashyap. And you will soon start your journey towards Bodhisattva." The old monk smiled.

"I think you have some confusion, sir. I'm still not accepting that you are the same MMK. I have no preconceived notions. Even I don't believe in these Maitreya things."

"You said it, Anand Kumar. No past and no future." The old man smiled again.

"I think you are playing with my mind. Or you are in my mind."

"Yet you followed my advice. Helped monk Kashyap to get rid of his problem."

"I think whoever you are, you have great yogic powers. You should have contacted him directly and told him that he was being used by that Tibetan minister."

"He is following the scriptures. Can't accept a living being."

"Living being what you are! Who has been buried 2500 years ago."

"I'm not sure about time. But yes, my body was buried in the past."

"And what I am seeing is your soul."

"Not my soul. I am a soul in a subtle body, whose physical body has been buried. But I know you are not going to believe. When you have some out-of-body experience, you will start believing."

"Again, I understand what you say. But only as a theory. For me, it is some kind of hypnotism." And please tell about my previous incarnation. You have been saying that I met Buddha in my previous birth as Upaka."

"Keep trying to remember. I never said you were Upaka. The person who met Tathagat isn't him. I hope you will be able to recall one day." He smiled.

Now again I had the same feeling I had earlier. He was going to depart. Soon I would come out of my deep slumber. Then I would start judging my experience.

I would find that the room is still locked from the inside. I would try to find a logical reasoning. I would try to convince myself that my unconscious mind was creating stories. This struggle would continue until my logical mind gives up.

THE END

www.ingramcontent.com/pod-product-compliance
Lightning Source LLC
La Vergne TN
LVHW091054150826
845673LV00002B/574